FIRE BREATHING OVIDE

Dragons of the Bayou

CANDACE AYERS

Lovestruck Romance Publishing, LLC

Ovide lost his mate years ago. Now, he's just biding time until his own demise which, thankfully, will come soon. The eclipse leading him to a slow descent into sweet oblivion is just around the corner.

Margo has never found a man who was worth the risk of heartbreak. No problem, because her caustic demeanor and sharp tongue scare away even the most persistent suitors.

When an accidentally-on-purpose claiming mark links them for all of eternity, both will have to rethink their plans for the future. But with the protective walls these two have constructed around their hearts, can they even expect to have a future together?

Chapter One

MARGO

"This section is closed." I called out to the asshat who was trying to pry open the old barn door separating the main part of my bar from the private party room in the rear.

The music was beating out a rhythm in the rest of the place, so I yelled to be heard over the thundering beat, then went back to scrolling my cell phone.

While I had a minute or two alone, which was rare, I was scanning a dating app for potential candidates. Unfortunately, there seemed to be a scarcity of men worthy of my consideration, which was odd since I wasn't looking for a romance book cover model or anything. Just an average, everyday Joe. I didn't need a muscled hunk, but I didn't want a guy whose face resembled a dog's butt either. Okay-looking, non-creepy, and someone who would accept a one-nighter as just one night —was that too much to ask? Oh yeah, no stalker tendencies either.

For a second, I thought about adding "someone my heart wouldn't get involved with" to the list, but that was entirely unnecessary. My heart was never involved. Never. I was pretty sure I wasn't capable of loving a man wholeheartedly. And there was a perfectly reasonable explanation for that. But I didn't care to expound upon my daddy issues.

At this stage in the game, though, my heart didn't need to be involved in sex. In fact, I preferred that the fist-sized organ behind my rib cage stay entirely out of my sex life (or lack thereof).

All I wanted to do was get laid.

At my age, even though nobody knew about it, being a virgin was no longer chaste or respectable. It was strange and put you in a category that included uptight prude, crazy cat lady and religious fanatic. In order to prove to myself that I wasn't any of those things, I only needed one night and a conscious, willing, not-hideous-looking man. Hell, I didn't even need a night. Twenty minutes or so would do.

As I scanned for a 'swipe right' candidate, the idiot on the other side of the door yanked again. This time so hard I thought that whoever it was out there might snap the thick iron bar that that ran the length of the doors bolting them closed.

I dropped my phone on a banquet table and stormed towards the doors. While my demeanor could never be described as naturally sunny, I was hosting a bachelor/bachelorette party for Lennox and Remy, and I was a little stressed. Wanting the party to go off without a hitch had raised my anxiety level to poking-a-bear.

"Hey, moron, if you don't quit jiggling that door, you're gonna find yourself trying to jiggle your head out of your sphincter.

I unlatched the bolt, yanked the door open, and came face to chest with Lennox's soon-to-be hubby, Remy.

"The hell, Remy? You trying to become the victim of a justifiable homicide? How would I explain that to Lennox? Why are you here, anyway? The party doesn't start for four more hours."

He grinned down at me and patted me on the head like I was a cocker spaniel. I played along and snapped at his hand which he moved out of range of my gnashing teeth just in time. "I have a delivery from my mate. Items for the party."

I accepted the bag he was carrying, but when I looked inside, I was baffled. "What the fuck is this?"

He shrugged and feigned innocence. "This wedding is making my female a little nervous."

I pulled out a jug of pickles and a roll of duct tape. "Okay, but what is this? What does she want me to do with it?"

He shook his head and held his palms up in front of him in the universal sign of surrender. "I am simply the messenger. I just deliver what I am told to deliver. I do not even understand this wedding tradition. I find it ridiculous."

"Don't let Lenni hear you say that." I reached into the bag again and pulled out a stack of wash clothes and a pack of gum. "Alright, seriously? Just take the whole bag back home with you."

"Ha!" He barked a laugh. "And face the wrath of my mate when she finds I did not deliver the items? You keep it here." He looked around. "Are you in need of assistance?"

I looked at a banner on the ground and nodded. "You can hang that for me."

He laughed. "I did not mean myself. I will send others to help. I am going back home to snuggle with my mate for a bit. There has been so much chaos with this ridiculous wedding tradition, she has had little time for more pleasurable pursuits."

I scowled at him and jerked my head towards the door, pleased for my bestie but a little envious of her, too. "Git, then, you useless dragon-man."

Just then my bartender, Sara, peeked in. "Ryan just called off. He broke his foot skateboarding this morning. And sorry, but I can't stay late today. I have that Tupperware party with my mom. If I cancel, she'll disown me." Sara spoke with just her head poking into the room, using the door to shield her body like she was afraid the news would push me over the edge and she needed to protect her vital organs. Sheesh.

"You're kidding me."

"I wish I was. I tried calling Marty but he's not answering."

I growled. "It's fine. I'll close the rest of the bar for a few hours if I have to."

"Remember what we talked about regarding you hiring more people? Not to say I told you so or anything, but we could really use extra help for times like this. You can't do everything all on your own, you know."

"Finish your shift and go home, Sara. And don't lecture me. I'm your boss."

Her head disappeared again but only for a second. "Margo! Fight!" Sara yelled through the barn door that was still slightly ajar.

I tucked my hair behind my ears and elbowed Remy out of the way. At five feet tall, maybe I should've had a hard time crossing a barroom tightly packed with people, but I didn't. I was quite skilled at handling my bar patrons. Of course, the heavy boots I wore helped. They gave me a few inches and could wield some painful kicks if I needed them to. I was also a ninja with the elbows.

I maneuvered my way to the fight—a tussle between two of my regulars—grabbed one of the men by the back of the shirt, yanking him back and then shoved my fingers into the neck of the man still trying to approach. "Knock it off! You want to keep drinking here, you knock it the fuck off!"

Jeff, the man struggling to get his shirt out of my iron grip, growled. "He started it."

Mark, coughing and sputtering, was smart enough to say nothing. He was too busy holding his throat and trying to get his breath back.

"Sort it out peacefully or find somewhere else to drown your sorrows, boys. You damage my bar and I'm going to cut your ball sacks off—the both of you! I don't pay a mortgage on this place for you two to go around breaking shit. I'm hosting a private party here tonight. If either of you boneheads give me grief, you won't need to worry about each other, I'll fuck ya' both up."

No need to stick around to see if they behaved themselves. I saw by their relaxed posture that neither was hankering for any more trouble. I turned and almost bumped into Remy. He must have thought I would need backup. Silly dragon. Not with those Bozos. Remy followed me to the back room and whistled approvingly. "Well done."

I hid a smile. "Go on, get out of here or I'll make you stay and help."

He held up his hands and backed away. "I will send help."

"You better." I turned to stare him down, but he was already gone, leaving me alone in the room. I eyed the banner on the floor mentally assuring myself that the night was going to be a success.

Lennox was finally getting a wedding of her dreams to the man of her dreams, the man she deserved. No more bullshit engagement to a philandering dickhead with an uptight nose-in-the-air family who wasn't fit to kiss the ground she walked on.

As for me, I would have to be content to live vicariously through her. At least one of us would get a happily ever after. I picked up my phone and continued scrolling through the dating app.

Chapter Two
OVIDE

Night was descending on Ferrer's Corner, the tiny town I'd resided in for the last seventy-five years. The place had once been home to a lively, small but growing community until the cannery closed. After that, the residents who were still of working age left, little by little, gone in search of jobs, and they'd taken their families along with them. Now, it was an old relic full of equally as old humans. And me.

The sun had set, which meant it was past bedtime for almost every resident in Ferrer's Corner. I hardly slept. Throughout the nights, I prowled the quiet town alone. Sometimes I merely sat perched on the edge of the town's fountain and watched the stars. They shone brighter near my cabin, but I felt a kinship with the cracked old fountain in the town square that still sputtered and spat water, albeit half the volume it once handled. I liked the *gurgle* of it. And, like me, it was old and broken yet still managed to rise in the morning and run its paces.

I sat perched in my human form tonight, listening to the bullfrogs whose croaks came closer at night.

Ferrer's Corner would soon fade to nothing with the passing of its current residents. The cookie cutter clapboard homes, the sparse general store, the barbershop that doubled as a gossip mill, and the little diner I often frequented would eventually crumble to the earth.

The fountain would eventually give up its sputtering, too. Thankfully, I would not be there to witness its demise.

My time was mercifully coming to an end. I sighed and stared at the blackening sky. I wondered what had become of the old world. Wyvern, our planet, was not yet visible in the sky from Earth, although it soon would be, as the eclipse neared.

Everything I had ever loved and cared about I'd left behind in Wyvern, buried in its moist, tepid soil. Not for the for the first time, not even for the thousandth, I wondered if I shouldn't have just remained there to be slain, my body left to rot alongside those who had meant the most to me.

Instead, I'd listened to Cezar's urging when he'd pleaded for my help. It had been his idea for those of us, the strongest, bravest warriors in each kingdom to sacrificially search out a new world. The irony of the situation was that when we returned to usher our people to safety in this world we'd discovered, we'd found that the slayers had already slaughtered and decimated our race. We were the only ones left.

The others convinced me that we had no choice but to flee. Why I listened rather than staying and accepting my fate of being slain and buried along with my kinsmen is a question I had pondered every day since.

I supposed I possessed a stronger will, a stronger force that urged a warrior such as myself to fight to survive, even when all he wanted to do was roll over and give up.

"Boy, you look more like a gargoyle than a dragon perched on the fountain like that every evening." Lonny, the owner of Main Street Diner, stepped out into the night air and locked the door behind herself. Her silver-white hair was dyed a bluish shade and she was dressed in her usual uniform of a brown and beige polyester dress which she accessorized with support hose and white orthopedic shoes. When her eyes met mine, she shook her head as though she disapproved.

I just shrugged. She was the only local who knew my secret. She'd waitressed at the diner for thirty years before she bought it from the previous owner and had watched me appear to defy age while she grew older. Oddly, she was the only town resident who seemed to notice. We had an unspoken agreement, she and I. I accepted her jabs in exchange for her delicious meals.

"Why don't you go out and do something?"

"Like what?"

She chuckled. "Don't make me spell it out for you, boy. Go out and find yourself a woman. For a night or for a week, whatever."

I looked away, not only embarrassed but disgusted at the idea of having sexual intercourse.

"Well, I'll be damned. Big dragon-men can blush." She patted my cheek with her knobby fingers and backed away. In her late seventies, she was as agile and graceful as ever. "Just go on. A handsome man like you should have no problem finding yourself a little poontang pie."

"Ugh!" I hung my head slapping a hand to my forehead. "Do me a favor and never use that term again. Ever."

She just laughed. "I'm sick and tired of you moping and brooding around here. You just need to...let's see...bump uglies, knock boots, get your freak on, however you want me to phrase it."

I cleared my throat loudly. "This conversation is over. I will see you tomorrow."

Fortunately, Lonny didn't press the issue. "Breakfast, as always."

I watched her until she was tucked away inside the small house just next door to her diner. After her kitchen light came on and I could hear her shouting at her husband, I was satisfied to look away.

As much as she would hate it if she knew, I'd made it my responsibility to look after her. Maybe that was the reason I was still alive. To make sure she was safe. I'd known her since she was a girl, fresh-faced and head over heels in love with Louis, the male she was now inside shouting at. Louis had grown hard of hearing over the years.

You will be attending the party this evening, correct? Remy 's words invaded my thoughts.

What party? I should have simply responded in the negative. To say I was not a party goer was an understatement.

The party that will be for both Lenni and me together. It is a human tradition to have a celebration before the mating ceremony. A party called a bachelor and bachelorette party. Our human mating ceremony is tomorrow. Have you forgotten?

I closed my eyes and squeezed the bridge of my nose. *No. I am simply doing something else at the moment.*

You are doing nothing but making excuses. You must come to our party tonight and to our ceremony tomorrow. We are a family, Ovide. Act like it. His thoughts were just a growl of frustration.

I was frustrated, too. I had no desire to attend a human mating ceremony. Nor did I care to be around newly mated, blissfully happy couples. I was slightly ashamed for wanting to avoid the only kinsmen I had, but it was misery to face all of them with their mates and their growing families—things I could never hope to have. *I am busy.*

You will come or I will send the others to retrieve you. He gave me the bar's name—The Gator Pit—and the location before barking at me once again to show up.

I had every intention of ignoring him, but within minutes, the other dragons were raising a cacophony inside my head and I agreed to go just to shut them the hell up.

It was the last thing I wanted to do—sitting at a table watching the others revel in the joy I had been cheated out of. It had been bad enough joining Armand and some of the others as they frequented bars looking for mates and pretending that I, too, was actively searching. Now that they had all found their females, why would they not just leave me alone?

I sighed in resignation as I roused myself off the ledge of the fountain to head home and shower before flying towards the party location. If I was lucky, I could put in a few minutes and then get the hell out of there.

Chapter Three

MARGO

Closing the bar for the party had been the best idea ever. It was a loss of revenue, but I figured I'd come up with a couple of promo ideas later in the month to draw a crowd—maybe a trivia night, or an 80's night, or dart tournament or something. My immediate priority was making sure the night was perfect for Lenni. And without the added chance of something stupid drawing me away and throwing off her party, I felt calmer. Somewhat.

"Holy guacamole, you didn't have to do all of this, Margo." Lenni looked around at the decorated back room, complete with colored lights and a disco ball, grinning like a Cheshire cat. Sky had shown up a few hours early to help with the set-up.

I'd gone with a black and gold motif and we'd decked the place out: garlands and streamers and banners, and just for a laugh, I included a bit of raunchiness. Lennox's eyes widened as she took in the penis straws, giant mylar penis balloons, and the array of sexually suggestive games and party decor strewn about the room. I'd even cleverly paired the normal balloons into sets of two, tips out.

I took her hands and smiled. "You deserve it. I hope it's a memory you keep forever." I meant that. It was good to know she was with a man who treated her right. Dragon, whatever.

"I have no doubt that will be the case! It's hilarious. You are so good at putting together a good time."

Nance placed a crown of plastic penises and brightly colored feathers on Lenni's head and spun her to face us. "And the raunch factor, I gotta tell you, A+ on that, Margo." Nance, the other of our trio of besties, pulled her own festive necklace over her head—big plastic boobs hanging from a chain.

"Are there penises on my head? There are penises on my head, aren't there?" Lenni giggled and squealed when she reached up and touched one of the rubber shafts. She released it as though it burned her fingers. "Oh, god!"

Lenni and Nance and I had been best friends since the first day of kindergarten. The two of them were pretty much the extent of my adult friends, which I'd convinced myself wasn't as pathetic as it sounded because I didn't have time to socialize anyway. Running a business kept me busy sixteen hours a day, seven days a week.

Nance and I exchanged glances before she dropped the bomb. "And the best and final surprise is...we invited your mother!"

The look of horror on Lennox's face had me nearly doubling over in laughter. "She's kidding!"

"Ugh, not even a little bit funny you two. I was this close to coming down with a last-minute case of bubonic plague."

Across the room, I caught Remy out of the corner of my eye as he held up a male blowup doll. His expression held a look of confusion mixed with horror as he stared at its plastic smile and full erection. Although he didn't say anything aloud, we read his lips as he mouthed, "What. Is. This?"

The three of us fell into a fit of hysterical giggles.

I left my girls to get back to work making sure everyone got settled in okay. I kept catching the dragons' reactions to the bawdy and vulgar sexual things strewn around the room and had to bite back more laughter especially when I overheard the group discussing their conclusion that the party must be some sort of human fertility ceremony.

I'd met almost all of the dragon gang since Lenni and Remy had gotten together. Remy 's twin, Blaise and his mate, Chyna. Chyna's twin, Cherry and her mate, Cezar. So many twins in the group. Sky and her mate, Beast. Armand and his mate Angel, who I'd just met about a week earlier.

As everyone began to settle into seats around the banquet table, I noticed there was one seat still vacant. I looked around, trying to figure out if I'd miscounted.

Angel saw my look and smiled. "Ovide."

"Is he coming?"

She shrugged. "The guys tried to talk him into it, but who knows if he'll actually show."

Lenni leaned over. "What are you two whispering about?"

"I was just wondering if Ovide was coming." I stepped back from the table and grinned at her. "Either way, it should be about time for dinner to be served. I'll be right back."

I walked through the main bar and into the kitchen to check on my cook, Aaron. "How's it coming, Aaron?"

He flashed a charming grin. "Four and a half minutes and I'll have the main course completely plated up. Need help serving it, gorgeous?"

"I'll manage." Aaron was always flirting with me and he made it very clear that the flirting was not all just fun and games. He'd be very open to taking our boss/employee relationship to a more personal level. I even thought of taking him up on it to solve my little V dilemma. The problem was, he was a great cook and a great employee and getting involved was a recipe for disaster. "I'll just make multiple trips. Thanks for the offer, though."

"Anything for you, Margo. And I do mean *anything*." He winked and I rolled my eyes.

I carried in bread baskets, depositing them on the table and refilled drinks before going back for the main course. I was acting as waitress, bartender, hostess, and all-around party coordinator for the night, and as someone who had a hard time sitting still, I was totally in my element.

I'd been working since I could remember—long before I was legal. In fifth grade, Mr. Fong who owned the local superette hired me to come in after school and on weekends to sweep floors and stock shelves. I was paid six dollars an hour under the table, which bought my mom and I clothes, toilet paper and other essentials not covered by food stamps. Working until exhaustion every night was still a comfortable feeling for me.

I balanced both trays of food to transport them to the guests in the private party room, but before I took two steps, I heard a knock at the back door. The back door opened into an alley and we'd told everyone arriving for the party to use that door to avoid any stragglers coming in with them, thinking the bar was open for business. I put the trays of food down and moved to the door to open it.

As soon as my hand gripped the doorknob, my heart sped up and I felt the weirdest thing. I could only describe it as an electric current buzzing through my body. It was so pronounced that my fight or flight instincts kicked in. Well, fight instinct. I'd never had a flight instinct.

Straightening my shoulders, I yanked open the door to face whatever or whomever was causing my body to react so strangely. I came face to chest with the missing dragon.

I knew instinctually that the hunky mountain of a man I was looking at was Ovide. There was no way the dark haired, dark eyed beefcake was not a shifter. He was too damned big, too damned muscled and too damned hot.

I gripped the doorknob hard to steady myself and tilted my chin up to take him in. Good god. Sexual energy radiated off the man in waves and the way those waves were slapping against my shore, I was lucky to still be on my feet. My body responded, my hip curving out just a bit more, my back arching slightly to reveal just a bit more of my cleavage.

"Ovide!" Sky appeared over my shoulder, shocking me back to reality. "You made it! We're glad you're here."

I snapped back to reality and stepped out of the way to let the man enter, but I couldn't keep my eyes from trailing his movements as he did. Shit, he was tall and broad. Like all of the dragons, he was big enough to intimidate any human man around. Clearly, he was a solid wall of testosterone, but his posture was unassuming. The unassuming stance did little to hide the tremendous power he held. He walked with his head ducked just slightly, so when he looked at me, it was through thick, dark lashes. His big hands shoved in his pockets, I couldn't help noticing the way his pants were pulled tight across the bulge in them.

"Margo?"

I blinked and forced myself to look away from Ovide's bulge. "Huh?"

Sky grinned. "I asked if you needed help serving the food."

I nodded and a sly smile spread over my face as I winked at Ovide. I'd never been accused of being shy. "It's Ovide, right? I could use some muscle and it looks like you're overflowing with it. Why don't you help a girl out? These trays are oh, so heavy."

Sky giggled and held up her hands. "I can take a hint. I'll leave you two to it."

Ovide looked stunned. I could see the heat in his eyes, but he also looked a little confused and a bit like a deer caught in headlights.

"I'm Margo. This is my bar, The Gator Pit." I motioned him over and pointed to the loaded trays.

He didn't move, though and his eyes remained focused on me. After a second or two, he cleared his throat and nodded. "Hello, Margo."

His voice was deep and bold but velvety and I felt my knees go weak at the sound. If I had drawn up an image of the perfect man, he would've looked and sounded exactly like Ovide. "Well, it's nice to meet you. I haven't seen you around with the rest of the dragon gang before."

Ovide finally pulled his eyes away from mine, noticed the trays laden with steaming dinnerplates, and stepped forward. "I do not get out much."

I grinned over at him and nodded towards the room where the others were waiting on their meals. "I can appreciate that. You can carry those on in. I'll be right behind you."

He picked up both trays like they weighed nothing and sauntered away from me. His eyes kept jumping back to me, though. The confusion in them seemed to intensify. He wasn't the first man I'd thrown off.

As soon as he was out of sight, I fanned myself. "Sweet Jesus, that is one red-hot dragon."

Chapter Four

MARGO

From what I could tell, everyone was enjoying their dinner and drinks. I sat back down next to Lenni, again surveying the room. They all talked and laughed together, enjoying each other's company. That was good. It was nice to see the group having so much fun together. I could appreciate their joy, but for me, the anxious energy I'd had that the party would go smoothly had turned into a raging attraction to the huge dragon at the end. It was hard to not look down the table at him. It seemed like he was having the same trouble. I kept catching his glances. Apparently, he wasn't too shy either, because he didn't seem to mind being caught staring—until I winked. Then, he looked away quickly and his brow furrowed in consternation.

"The big hottie keeps checking you out." Nance, on my other side, elbowed me. "Looks like maybe you found yourself a wedding hookup."

Ovide coughed and I knew that he'd heard. I leaned into Nance and whispered loudly, "I wouldn't hesitate to eat cake off of him."

I felt a little wild and uninhibited as we both laughed. I was drunk on the attraction. It was exhilarating but potent. I couldn't remember the last time I'd been so attracted to a man. Oh, wait, yes I could. That would be—never! Of course, with the exception of the bar, like Ovide,

I didn't get out much either. So, the men in my life were pretty much steady drunks, on a bender, or just hanging at my bar nursing drinks to avoid wives or girlfriends.

I looked back down at Ovide to find him again staring at me, his eyes glowing more golden than brown. I watched as he licked his lips and *felt* his growl more than heard it—right down between my legs. The idea of crawling down the table to straddle him right then there, in front of everyone, crossed my mind.

"This is delicious, Margo."

I jerked my eyes to Cherry and smiled. "I wish I could take credit. I can't cook at all. I'll pass the compliment to Aaron, though."

"Don't. He already thinks he's God's gift to the human race." Nance rolled her eyes. "For some unknown reason."

"Be nice."

"No way. He's a creep, always hitting on you"

Suddenly, the chatter at the table stopped abruptly as a low growl echoed through the room. All eyes turned to Ovide. When he realized, his growling ceased abruptly, and he stared down every set of eyes until, one by one, they looked away and resumed eating.

"Anyhoo," Nance continued. "He's always coming onto you. It's creepy. He needs to take a hint. But, these potatoes are delicious."

"I can handle him just fine."

"Does he actually bother you?" Angel asked

"No. If he did, he'd be fired." I held up my fork to Nance. "Now, you stop it. Behave, or you'll be the one playing unicorn for the game later tonight."

Before I served the cake, I brought out more drinks as people needed them and took away dinner plates. I had to lean over Ovide to put his drink down in front of him, and when the side of my breast brushed him, the sensation that sparked through me was insane. It made the food tasteless. I was too distracted by the tingly buzz flowing in my veins.

I leaned down so my face was near his ear and spoke before I knew what was coming out of my mouth. "The offer with the cake still stands." His grin was wide and mesmerizing, a flash of gleaming, pearly white that lit up his face and sent tingles straight to my lady parts. "No hands." I waggled my brows.

Ovide straightened, eyes focused ahead, then suddenly he threw back his head and deep, rich laughter echoed throughout the room.

I grinned like he and I were in our own little world until I noticed that the rest of the room was frozen solid—like statues carved in stone. The entire room—silent. Forks were poised halfway to mouths and jaws were dropped open in what looked like stunned amazement, eyes were bugging out. What the hell was everyone was staring at? Had they never seen or heard the guy laugh before?

Apparently not, because it wasn't until Cezar cleared his throat loudly that the rest of the dragon gang appeared to remember themselves and all looked away trying to fake normalcy. I heard them, though. Little titters expressing shock that Ovide's face hadn't cracked into a million pieces.

I ignored them and sauntered back to my seat blowing out a deep breath. Ovide was hot enough to burn me, but I wanted to throw myself at him, anyway. He was definite swipe right material.

After dinner, a few of us got up to use the restroom and to stretch our legs before games and gifts. I leaned my shoulder against the wall next to Nance and faced her, away from Ovide. "Men shouldn't be that hot, Nance."

She raised a brow. "Yet, there he is."

"I need a bag of ice, a fan, and some hormone suppressants to get through this party." I squirmed. "And dry panties."

She laughed out loud and shook her head at me. "Judging by the way he's looking at your ass right now, I'd say you might as well save yourself the effort and ditch the panties altogether."

Like a couple of teenagers, we giggled and high fived each other. I calmed down first and pushed my hair out of my face. "Okay. I've got to finish this party without making a slobbering fool of myself."

Easier said than done, considering the games I had planned for the rest of the night. A suck and blow game with a large straw and a bowl of grapes, a pin the condom on the chin dildo game, and a game of truth or dare—lord, keep me from embarrassing the hell out of myself.

My fears of embarrassing myself turned out to be unfounded,

though. Just when everyone was getting ready to play the suck and blow game, Chyna released a piercing squeal of pain. She clutched at her huge, pregnant belly as a puddle of fluid gathered at her feet.

Blaise let out a scream that was oddly high pitched for a huge dragon. "It's time!"

Chyna waved him away, her face still clenched in pain. "No, no. It's fine. Let's finish the party!"

Lenni waved her hands back and forth frantically. "No! You're having a baby! This is so exciting!"

"But Margo worked so hard..."

I shook my head. "Girl, you can't stop a baby from coming. Besides, I'm more than happy to kick most of y'all out and spend the rest of the night relaxing."

"Most of us, huh?" Nance nudged me and grinned.

"Everyone, move! I must transport my female to the hospital!" Blaise was pale and wide-eyed and looked as though he was on the verge of passing out.

"Blaise. Home birth. We discussed this. Take me home." Chyna rolled her eyes and then cried out again. "Take me home, now!"

Everyone gathered up their belongings in a rush, amidst an air of excitement. Soon they'd be welcoming another little one to their group. Lenni paused to give me a tight hug, thank me for all my hard work, and to tell me she'd see me in the morning.

Ovide hadn't moved. Like a beacon in the night, I couldn't help noticing. He stood perfectly still, watching me as others shuffled and moved around us until finally when the two of us were alone, he spoke.

"I will help clean."

Four words had never sounded so good.

Chapter Five
OVIDE

As I cleared the half empty cake plates from the table and stacked them on trays, I watched Margo from the corner of my eye. I had no idea what force had overcome me. Never in all my days had I had a reaction to a female like the one I was having to the petite female with the flame colored hair and lively green eyes. In fact, with the exception of Kyrian, I'd never had a reaction to a female at all. Even with Kyrian, I hadn't had such an extreme response.

Now, my body was reacting to Margo as though she was...was... my *mate*—completely forgetting that I had once had a true mate whom I'd almost claimed. My foolish dragon was fighting to get to the tiny redhead, to sink his teeth in and render a claiming mark on her creamy, snow white flesh.

When Lonny had suggested earlier that I find comfort with a female, I hadn't bothered to explain that I'd never before lain with a female. Kyrian and I had planned to mate as soon as we came of age but our plans were thwarted by her sudden illness. She'd gone fast, and ever since Kyrian died, the mere thought of being with another female was not only uncomfortable, it was stomach-turning and vile.

Until now.

I knew by the way Margo was toying with me, sending me heated looks and whispering in my ear, that the feelings between us were mutual. I could smell her arousal, and the sweet aroma of her affected me like the strongest aphrodisiac. I also knew Remy claimed she was a witch. Had she cast a spell on me?

I wanted her, yet... that part of me that belonged to Kyrian fought savagely. Both sides of me battling, and my dragon, well, he had a mind of his own.

Whenever Margo got too close to me, I moved away, picking up trash, sweeping, collecting plates. I was confused and conflicted by what was happening. Even with the lust deafening the guilt, it was still there, nagging at the back of my brain. I needed to go, but with every second that passed...I just...couldn't remember why I needed to go.

"So, that thing about eating cake?" She waggled her eyebrows at me. "You interested?"

I had stayed after the others left for only two reasons. One, my dragon would not allow me to leave, and two, because I did not want that fucker Aaron anywhere near Margo. But that was all.

I could not allow anything else to occur between us.

"No, I am not interested in a relationship."

"Relationship?! Who said anything about a relationship? I just want a good fuck."

"I am not interested in a fuck either."

She looked crestfallen and I immediately felt guilty.

She held up her hands in surrender. "Fine. Okay. Whatever. I guess I misread the signals. Completely and totally. I thought you wanted me, too."

I nodded curtly, but she had not misread. I did want her.

While I finished sweeping, she picked up her phone. "I guess it's back to searching for Mr. Swipe Right."

Mr. Swipe Right? Yes, fine.

After several minutes, I could not let it go. I had to know. "Who is this Mr. Swipe Right you are searching for?"

Her laugh was more a snort through her nose than a laugh. "It's not a *who*. It's an app. A dating app."

I knew all about such things from Cezar. Before he met Cherry, he'd had the idea to search dating sites and dating aps to find a mate.

As the thought sank in, I realized she was looking for a stranger on a dating site to copulate with. The thought horrified me.

She must have read my expression. "Don't look so freaked out. It wouldn't be anything serious. Just looking to get my groove on if you know what I mean."

I knew what she meant. I knew and I didn't like it at all. "So you are planning to put your *groove* on a male who is a complete stranger?"

"Um, yeah, that's the point—a hookup with no strings."

My eyes darkened and I could barely suppress a growl. "That does not sound safe."

"Well, I'd take precautions. You know, do an internet search, tell someone where I was, use condoms. Besides, I can take care of myself."

I wondered about that.

"So, you will simply find a random stranger, and have sexual intercourse with him?"

I was becoming angrier by the second. The thought of her being so careless with her safety irked me. But, what could I do? I could offer to stand guard outside the bedroom door, but the thought of another male putting put his hands on her delectable curves, or his mouth on her luscious pink lips was infuriating.

"Hey, listen buddy, no slut shaming. I'm a grown woman. I have every right to have 'sexual intercourse' with whoever I want."

I grunted. She wanted a male whose aim was nothing more than to achieve his own pleasure and then walk away. I was livid at the thought of a male regarding her that way. Before I knew it, I heard a crack.

"Hey! You broke my barstool! What the hell, Ovide?!"

I looked down to find myself holding half of the seat portion of one of the barstools in my fist. "I-I am sorry," I growled out. I was not sorry at all.

She pointed her finger at me emphatically. "You're buying me another one of those."

I narrowed my eyes at her and glowered.

"What the fuck? You're looking at me like you want to go all warrior dragon on my ass."

I wanted to go something on her ass, but it had nothing to do with fighting. I could not get the thought of her in the arms of another off my mind. My pulse raced.

"Alright, you're acting all wigged out. I think you should just get out of here. We're just about done anyway. I can finish up myself. Thanks for staying and helping me out."

"I am not leaving."

"Well then, what the fuck's your problem?"

"I will tell you what the fuck my problem is. The thought of you with another male makes my blood boil."

Her jaw dropped. I had clearly surprised her. "Why?"

"Because!"

Her voice became breathier. "Because why?"

I growled again and took several steps forward until I was inches from her. With a finger under her chin, I tilted her head up to meet my gaze and surprised even myself with the words that tumbled from my lips.

"Because I want that male to be me."

Chapter Six
OVIDE

Her eyes focused on my mouth, she bit her lip and her fingers grasped the front of my shirt. She may have figured on doing this with some slimy male on some slimy app but I could not allow that.

"Oh, uh...o-kay then."

"Okay then." I nodded sharply. "I want to kiss you."

She did not hesitate. "Do it."

I paused for only a moment, a niggling at the back of my mind telling me that there was something else—something I was to consider. Perhaps some reason for caution. But, when she wrapped her arms around my neck pulling my mouth to hers, a fire ignited between us and I found my blood being heated to an inferno by the firecracker in my arms.

When I lightly pressed my lips to hers, the moan she released was the most deliciously erotic sound I have ever heard. The kiss was over in seconds as I pulled away to judge her reaction.

I did not release my grip on her, but she did not attempt to move away either. She merely looked up at me with those enchantingly emerald eyes, her lips parted. I needed to kiss her again. This time to take possession of her. I needed to hear the sound of her little moan of pleasure again. *Needed* as in a powerful, overwhelming, primal urge. I drew her small frame tighter into me and tilted her head so as to have the perfect angle of her mouth to mine.

This time, my lips played against hers, brushing lightly, and I reveled in the experience of breathing in her scent—pineapple and coconut—and enjoying the caress of her soft, full lips against my mouth. This time, I played against the seam of her full lips until they parted allowing my tongue to delve inside.

For every stroke of my tongue, every ounce of my passion, she matched me—ounce for ounce. It was not enough, though. I wanted, needed, more. Margo was one step ahead of me. She managed to climb me and lock her legs around my waist. When I straightened, our bodies rubbed together deliciously and I found my fingers digging into her soft ass, clenching her tighter against me.

She kissed me deeper, her teeth nipping at my lips. I gripped her ass harder and locked her body against mine as I growled into her kiss.

"Floor." She tried to untangle herself from me, but I was not letting her go. "Floor."

Before I could lower us to the floor, Margo pushed us off the wall and we went tumbling to the ground. I rolled so she was on top of me. It was an interestingly strategic move on her part, and apparently just what she had intended because she wore a wicked grin as she stared down at me.

"This has to go." Straddling my hips, she trailed her fingers down my chest and caught the hem of my shirt. Tugging it up, she tried to take it off of me. When I caught it and ripped it in two in an attempt to impress her, her eyes went wide and she wiggled herself against the bulge in my jeans. "Do mine, too."

Not needing to be told twice, I grabbed her shirt and shredded it. Her breasts were held in a silky undergarment that I wanted off. I lengthened my claws just enough to easily slice through the front so it fell open and her breasts bobbed out, full and creamy, topped with bright pink nipples that begged for my mouth.

"Hey! That was a good bra!"

I brushed my fingertips over one of her rosy pink nipples, watching it harden and tighten and and as her arousal perfumed the air, I took it in my mouth, rolling my tongue around it.

"Mmm...I'll forgive you this time, though."

As I feasted on her luscious breasts, her moans became more urgent. She clutched at my hair and worked her hips against mine.

Just when I thought I couldn't take any more, she pulled back and kissed down my neck, sinking her blunt little teeth into my chest, a move which spoke to my dragon. He was thrilled with the gesture—so close to that of a claiming mark—and it was all I could do to keep a reign on myself and to keep from shifting into my beast.

Margo's hands shook as she unbuttoned my pants and grunted in frustration when she couldn't get them down fast enough. Her impatience and eagerness worked against her as she struggled.

I took over, wrapping her tightly in my arms and rolling us, so she was under me.

The need to take possession of her was increasing as was my desire to hear more of her pleasured moans. I tore at her jeans and removed them along with her panties effortlessly until she was naked beneath me.

I wanted to devour her whole. Her delicious fragrance was the sweetest, most enticing scent I'd ever experienced. As I trailed kisses down her stomach, breathing her in, I stroked my fingers along the seam of her folds. A shiver ran through me when she adjusted herself so that her thighs opened more for me. I pressed my finger into her warm depths, sliding one into her core. She whimpered and my finger slid deeper.

"I want to taste you."

When Margo responded, her voice was just above a hoarse whisper. "Do it."

She was hot. And wet...and, I discovered as I lapped my tongue along the seam of her folds tasting her, sweet as honey. She truly tasted of the most delicious nectar as her juices flooded my taste buds. Never had I experienced such a tantalizing flavor. I licked her again and again, rolling my tongue around the small bud near the top of her folds. When her thighs trembled and she rocked against my mouth, her hands fisted in my hair, I felt a surge of pride.

My greatest joy was in watching her glean her pleasure and as I rolled my tongue in just the right spot, and she squirmed under me.

When her breathing quickened and her body began to tense, I buried my face between her thighs, licking and sucking her even harder until a small, breathy scream erupted from her throat and her body trembled in release. Exquisite—she was exquisite.

My cock felt as though it was made of the hardest marble. I could not keep my thoughts from escaping my mouth in a husky growl.

"I want to fuck you."

She met my gaze, her eyes heavy-lidded, her lips slightly parted, her breathing raspy. "Do it."

When I dragged the head of my cock against her dripping folds, she gasped.

"You're so big!" I detected a small amount of apprehension—perhaps fear—in her voice.

"Do you wish me to stop?" I was throbbing, wanting nothing more than to enter her waiting core, but her pleasure was my priority.

"No, no. It's just..." She covered her beautiful face with her hand as though she did not want to speak.

"Tell me."

"This is my first time, that's all. Go slow?"

I nodded. I was honored to be her first. It was an honor I did not take lightly. Not at all. "It is also my first time. I will let you lead."

She looked surprised, but only for a moment until I rolled us once again so that I was beneath her. She rose, undulating her hips against me. Her breasts jiggled enticingly as she moved, calling to me. While one hand remained on her hip, holding her steady, my other caressed her mounds, stroking and squeezing, toying with her, gently pinching her tightly puckered nipples.

Margo lined us up and slowly lowered herself on me. Very slowly. Excruciatingly slowly. My cock sank inch by inch into the hot, tight warmth of her and I could barely stand it. When I was almost a third of the way in, she stopped and took a deep breath. I was just about to ask her if she was okay when she slammed down hard onto me sinking until her ass hit my pelvis and she cried out in a mix of pleasure and pain. "Oh, fuck."

I froze, not wanting to add to any discomfort she might be feeling. I was beginning to wonder if she wanted to stop, but after a moment, she began rocking against me once more. Her pace was slow at first, then gained momentum.

She was the most beautiful sight I had ever seen in all my decades of existence as I watched her rock herself on my dick. I reached up and stroked my hand down the curve of her breast, her waist, her stomach, just reassuring myself that this beautiful creature was real, and not some sort of mystical hallucination.

She picked up her pace, her body clenching me so tightly my cock throbbed with the need to release. I stroked the small bud at the top of her folds which generated a loud moan and caused her hips to jerk in response.

"Firecracker," I murmured.

Her body fell forward so that with every rocking stroke as she slid up and down on me, her nipples tickled my chest. She shuddered violently, and this time when she rocked against me, I clasped her hips and dragged her down a little harder, trying to pull her deeper.

Margo moaned again, her body trembling. "That...that's...amazing."

And that is when it happened...

My fangs extended. I could feel my golden dragon just below the surface of my skin itching to emerge. My tongue licked the pale skin of her throat, preparing it for my sharp canines. Her enticing aroma swirled in my nostrils. When I spoke, my mouth against her flesh, my voice was little more than a growl. "I want to...I want to..."

Margo's lips were millimeters from my ear when she responded, sending goosebumps over my body.

"Do it."

Chapter Seven

MARGO

Any control I'd had—any reservation, and semblance of rational thought—vanished as Ovide's mouth was on my neck, his hot tongue stroking the tender skin there. I'd like to say that I didn't know what he meant when he growled out something virtually incoherent, or that I wasn't in control of my faculties when I answered him by saying, "Do it."

But, I did, and I was.

Any chance of holding off my orgasm flew out the window as his teeth sank into my neck. At the moment the first contractions of my orgasm began, the sharp bite took me to heights of pleasure I never before thought possible. My veins pumped furiously, a molten fire. My orgasm started at my core and tightened its way through my body. Feeling Ovide's teeth clasped onto my flesh, I let out a wild scream. He took me harder, on the verge of his own climax. I felt my blood filling his throat as his seed, hot and marking me as his, filled my core.

All I could do was hold onto him as each of us drew the essence of the other into our very being.

It was seconds...or minutes...or hours...before, trembling and still rocked with aftershocks of pleasure, I felt his teeth pull out of my neck and his tongue stroke over the mark. He pulled back enough to cup my face between his hands and kiss me tenderly. I tasted everything in that kiss. Me, him, us. It was slow and lazy, more of a promise than a demand.

His skin rippled; his dragon was close to the surface. I pulled back to look at him and witnessed golden dragon scales along his chest and biceps. Meeting his eyes, I was looking not into the eyes of the man, but of the dragon.

I rested my forehead against his, holding the dragon's gaze, and bit my lip. "Both of you are pretty fantastic."

I was rewarded with a little roar of pleasure and then a flash of long, sharp canines. When Ovide, the man, took over, he closed his eyes and held me tighter. I wanted to bathe in that embrace for the rest of my life—safe and comforted.

Still hard in me, Ovide moved again. Slow and steady, we rocked against each other, our foreheads still pressed together. A slow build, the next orgasms weren't any less significant. I didn't know how much time had passed. It ceased to exist or matter. There was just the strength of the connection between us.

Then suddenly, it was over.

The euphoria faded and reality came crashing through the blissed-out haze I was swimming in when I realized the implication of what the hell had just happened. A second later, Ovide's body tensed and I heard him inhale sharply. He must have come to the same realization I had.

I was, for once in my life, stunned speechless.

I pushed myself off of Ovide and rolled over so I was facing away from him as my brain fought to process the situation. He claimed me! He fucking marked me! And I all but begged him to do it! Oh, fuck me! I wanted to lie to myself and claim that I was human and had no idea what I'd been asking for when I egged him on, but it wasn't true. I knew exactly what a claiming mark was and how it was given.

Now what?

I felt awkward and uncomfortable. I didn't know what to do—or say—or even how I was supposed to feel. I was kind of wishing I would disappear, or Ovide would disappear. I needed space and time to think, to figure this out.

Curled up on the floor of the bar, I felt Ovide moving away and heard him dressing. My stomach tightened, somehow able to feel his emotional withdrawal. He was leaving. Good. Then I didn't have to confront the elephant in the room, or try to make small talk around it.

Once he was dressed, there was silence for several minutes. I imagined him standing there wracking his brain for something to say. The right words, perhaps, but were there any 'right words'?

In the end, he only uttered two. "I'm sorry."

His mumbled apology was little more than a whisper of air.

I wanted to say something in response, but what? Thanks for the good time? It's been real? See ya' 'round? Nothing seemed appropriate so I remained silent, listening as he hesitated before turning and leaving, closing the door behind him.

Phew. Okay, that was a relief.

Except, what had he meant by 'I'm sorry'? Sorry how? Sorry for what? Sorry he had sex with me? Sorry he was leaving? Sorry he listened to me when I told him to mark me? Sorry he met me? What the hell?

I had half a mind to call him and ask just what the fuck he was sorry about...

Except I was still laying on the floor naked, so I dragged my weakened, trembly-but-satiated body up to my feet and forced myself to get dressed. I still had the last bit of the bar to finish cleaning and I could hear the morning songbirds chirping outside. Great.

I made myself focus on getting the rest of the dishes into the dishwasher and starting it. I was exhausted, but I knew if I slowed down, I would keep obsessing on what the hell had just happened—or that damned apology.

By the time I left the bar and walked the two blocks to my apartment, the sun was up and shining brightly. It was going to be a beautiful day for Lenni and Remy's wedding. I had enough time to take a twenty minute power nap and then haul ass over to put the finishing touches on the venue for the midday event.

As soon as I got close, though, I spotted Lenni waiting at my front door.

"What are you doing here? Today's your wedding day. Why aren't you at home getting your beauty sleep or worrying it might rain or—"

"Rain? Oh my god, I hadn't thought about that! What of it rains? Everything is outdoors! It'll all be ruined!"

"Relax. I checked the forecast again an hour ago. Bright and sunny. Now what gives? Why are you here?"

"Oh. I came to tell you that Chyna and Blaise are now the parents of a beautiful baby girl who they named Destiny, and that we've decided to move the wedding to their backyard. The dragons are moving the big stuff right now."

Damn, that meant I'd have to call the caterer, the florist and the DJ and give everyone the new location, ASAP.

"And this." Lenni handed me a half-full, black plastic trash bag. "I also wanted to make sure you had this stuff for later."

I peeked into the bag which appeared to be loaded with seemingly random items. I reached in and pulled out a roll of tinfoil raising my brows questioningly.

"In case anyone wants to take home some wedding cake, duh."

I rolled my eyes. "Right. I'll be sure to pass it along to the caterers in case they happen to have a shortage," I answered dryly.

"Where were you anyway, Margo? You look rough." She stroked her hand over my hair and winced. Then, comprehension seemed to dawn and her face lit up. "Were you with Ovide? I saw the way you two were stalking each other last night. We all did. I gotta tell you, we were shocked to heck. None of us have ever heard Ovide belly laugh like that. I mean it was a complete anomaly."

I let us in and hurried into the bathroom. She was right. I did look rough. I reached into the shower and turned the water on. As steam started filling the room, I stared at my reflection.

"Are you okay?"

I blinked at the reflection staring back at me in the mirror. "Yeah, sorry. I'm just exhausted."

"Because of Ovide?" She grinned.

"I wasn't stalking him." I hadn't pushed him into sex, had I? No, he had certainly seemed willing enough.

"You two were eye-screwing each other, for sure. What happened? Did something go wrong?"

Still staring at my own reflection, I moved my hair to the side. Both of our gazes went to the mark that decorated my neck. When Lenni's gaze moved back to mine, her eyes had grown huge.

"That's a...that's a..." She was obviously excited by the news, but one more look into my eyes and she deflated. "Well, that complicates things."

I nodded and blew out a breath. "Yeah."

Chapter Eight
OVIDE

Sitting across from Lonny at the diner, I stared down at the plate of food she'd brought me. I did not know what to do. I was a shameful mess.

"Are you going to tell me what crawled up your ass and died or do I have to sit here and just imagine all the ways someone pissed in your cheerios?"

I let my head fall back and stared at the ceiling fan slowly whirling overhead. "I have made a terrible mistake. I have done something unforgiveable."

Understatement of the year. I had crossed lines that I could not uncross. I had lost control. Worse, my dragon had lost control and he did not give a damn. He'd marked the sexy little human and was demanding that she was our mate. Yet she could not be. Kyrian was my mate.

"Well, letting my food go cold isn't going to make it any better." She nodded to the plates of food in front of me piled high with eggs, bacon, sausage, ham, potatoes, and grits. "Eat and talk. The Sunday morning crowd will be here soon."

I shoveled something into my mouth and chewed. I didn't know what it was I was chewing. Everything was tasteless. Kyrian's face wasn't as solid in my memory as it had been the day before. Before Margo.

"I was with a female last night." As the words left my lips, I was overwhelmed with more shame and heartache.

"About damn time, too." She snorted. "You're a young man, or at least you look like a young man. You've been living like some broody nun for too damned long, if you ask me."

I shook my head and dropped the fork again, covering my face with my hands. "I am ashamed."

"Of what? Wait a minute. You didn't, you know, force her or anything, did you?"

I choked. "What?! Of course not. I'm not a monster!"

"Well, technically..."

I growled. "She was more than willing."

"Is she married?"

"No."

"Well? What is the problem? Why the shame? Is she your brother's girl, or something?"

"No. She is not committed to anyone." *Besides me, now.* "I...I am, though. Committed, I mean."

Lonny raised her eyebrows. "Not in the decades that I've known you. I would've noticed a Mrs. Dark and Gloomy."

"I am capable of eating you in one bite, old woman. You know that, right?"

"Ha! If you were into eating people, I doubt you'd choose a dried-up old prune like me."

I sighed. "In the old world, I had a mate."

She was silent for a moment before responding. "I see. And where is she? Did you leave her there?"

"In a sense." In her grave, next to my mother's. My chest ached as I tried to hold on to the feelings I'd carried for Kyrian for so many centuries. My dragon wasn't on board with my deep mourning anymore, though. He grew agitated, wanting instead to focus on Margo.

"Well?"

I looked into the intelligent, milky grey eyes across from me. Her face was lined with deep wrinkles from a life well lived.

"She died. Long ago. That doesn't mean I can just move on. Dragons mate once. Once and that is all. My mate died and I should have died with her or lived the rest of my days mourning her. Last night I... I made a huge mistake. Shamefully, I thought only of myself. I do not get to move on. I do not get to find another mate."

I half expected Lonny to chastise me, or criticize, or laugh, but I was wrong. She did none of those things. She merely stared at me thoughtfully for several seconds before replying. "But, you did."

I nodded. It had to be some kind of mistake. It should not have been possible.

"Here comes an early bird." Lonny stood up and rested her hand on my shoulder. "Life just happens the way it happens, Ovide. Sometimes we just can't make sense of the whys and wherefores. I do know one thing though. You can kick and scream or you can welcome the gifts life lays at your feet. Your choice."

I patted her hand and then went back to staring down at my plate. That might have been good advice for humans, but I was a dragon. There were centuries old laws of nature that applied to us. I could not just reset our laws of biological evolution.

We're moving the location of our mating ceremony. We will have it at Blaise's castle so Chyna can watch from the window with her new infant youngling. Remy's voice was every bit that of a proud uncle. *Be on time.*

Another lightning bolt of pain shot through me. Yet another young. A gift from the fates, one that I had given up hope of having a long time ago. Kyrian and I had talked about a family, but after her death, I hadn't thought much about it again. Now, for whatever reason, the idea once again made my pulse quicken with a longing and my traitorous mind strayed to what Margo would look like, her belly swollen with our young. Not Margo! I shut the thought down and squeezed my eyes shut. Kyrian was my mate.

With Kyrian gone, I was destined to be alone until death. Whatever had happened the night before had been a trick, a mistake. It could not be a real mating.

I bussed my own table, walking my plate back to the kitchen and grabbed a rag to wipe down the Formica tabletop as I always did.

When I left the diner, rather than having to face any of the humans in town, I walked back through the woods to my cabin and sat on the back porch facing the acres of woodland that I owned. It had once been an open field, until I'd planted the trees—each in memory of Kyrian.

The forest was a monument to my mate. In her memory, I planted a tree for every month since I'd last seen her. A little piece of myself was buried with each of the trees and the wooded area was something that I viewed with reverence—a living symbol of my loyalty to my mate, no matter how many centuries passed. Hundreds and hundreds of trees each grown from saplings, all cared for as I would have cared for my mate, had she survived.

Unlike the other dragons who had built massive castles with the hopes of one day pleasing their mates and filling their walls with young, I had built a simple log dwelling. As long as I'd been here, I had never harbored the hope of pleasing a mate or of hearing the laughter of my own young echo through my home.

I wondered now how Margo would view my home. Would it please her? Would she be disappointed with it?

Grunting in frustration, I rose to my feet. It did not matter what Margo thought. She would never step foot in my home. She was not my true mate.

Tense and at war within myself, I forced myself to look at each and every tree I could see from where I sat. Each one a visual reminder of time I spent grieving a loss and missing Kyrian. Everything had changed in a matter of hours.

Shame and guilt weighed heavily on my shoulders, and horror joined it as I tried to bring to mind Kyrian's face. Each time, the image of Kyrian's blond hair and blue eyes morphed into Margo's, with piercing green eyes and fiery red hair. Jumping up, I rushed into the house, determined to wash away the night before and forget it all. I would regain my loyalty to my mate. I would not replace her. I would not.

I scrubbed myself in the shower, visions of Margo taunting me.

Fighting them, I forced myself to recall time spent with Kyrian—all the dreams we'd had and plans for our future. Memories of wandering through the kingdom's gardens with my sweet, delicate, gentle Kyrian, holding each other under archways made of wildflowers suddenly turned into visions of a hard bar floor and a fierce, sassy female with wild eyes and a sharp tongue.

I hung my head as scalding water pounded my shoulders.

What had I done?

Chapter Nine

MARGO

Not sure if the dragon gang realized how much work it was to change wedding venues at the last minute. For me—how much work it was *for me*.

I balanced myself on the top of the ladder as I hung the last of the fairy lights. Mentally, I was checking off the do items on my list.

DJ – check.

Caterer – check.

Floral arrangements – check.

Canopy, tables, place settings – check.

Chairs – check.

Cezar was rolling out the white vinyl runner between the rows of folding chairs for the procession to use as an aisle. So, check.

Bartender – check.

I would have acted as bartender but I was maid of honor as well as wedding planner and coordinator, so I had other duties, besides the dragons only drank a special concoction. Something Armand brewed up in his at home workshop.

The only problem I could foresee was that the last-minute change didn't allow enough time for an exterminator to come out and spray. In Louisiana bayou country, that could prove to be a problem.

By the time I got everything set up and spent a few minutes holding Destiny, Chyna and Blaise's new little dragonette, it was time for me to get my bridesmaid dress on and get ready for the wedding. No nap, no time to adjust, just constant motion. That was a good thing. It helped keep my wandering mind off Ovide. A little.

Actually, not at all.

I knew the second Ovide arrived. I could feel it like a sixth sense. No, not like a sixth sense. More like an overdose of female Viagra. I wondered if he could sense me too. I mean, it had to be an effect of the claiming mark, so wouldn't he feel the same thing?

No time to think. Before I knew it, I was walking down the makeshift aisle, headed towards Blaise, who was officiating, and Remy who standing off to the side.

Blaise and Chyna's home was in the middle of a swamp, but there was a substantial area that I had completely transformed into a picture book setting. There were floral garlands weaving their way around every bench, table, and through the small pergola where the actual ceremony would take place. I'd had the florist place bouquets of fresh flowers on the tabletops and I'd strung fairy lights everywhere. Come evening, the place would look enchanting.

As I did the slow "wedding walk" down the aisle, I knew Ovide's eyes were on me and I knew like radar exactly where he was standing. I didn't look. I was too afraid of what I would see in his eyes.

Indifference? Regret? Disgust? I supposed it depended on what he'd meant when he'd said he was sorry earlier.

I reached the front of the aisle and stepped over to the side like I was supposed to and damned if I didn't look up and meet Ovide's eyes. We both looked away quickly.

I forced myself to focus on Lenni as she began her procession down the aisle looking every bit like a Disney princess. If I ever cried, I would have teared up at that moment. I wasn't a crier, though, not since childhood. Nance, on the other hand blew her nose so loudly she sounded like a bugle and she had streaks of mascara running down her cheeks.

I suddenly felt a little self-conscious standing in front of all of the dragons and their mates. Did everyone know?

My mind was so preoccupied with ignoring Ovide that I zoned out. I guess I missed most of the vows between Lenni and Remy, because when I tuned back in, I heard Remi saying, "...the most loved, the most cherished, forever."

The tail end of Remy's vows to my best friend hit me harder than they should have. Lenni sighed happily and they exchanged rings. I knew a bit about mates. I had a long-lost uncle that I had connected with a few years back who'd mated with a tiger shifter from Lafayette. But I'd never thought it would happen to me.

I was completely confused. The claiming mark certainly did complicate things, just like Lenni said. I meant it when I'd told Ovide that I didn't want a relationship. I had two close friends and my bar to keep my happy. That worked for me.

With Ovide's mark throbbing on my neck, however, my head was suddenly filling with frilly images of kids, a dog, a stupid big old farmhouse with the laughter of playing, running children echoing off the walls. Things I'd been perfectly happy without—until now. One night with Ovide and I couldn't help but wonder. Worse—hope.

I caught Ovide's eye again and held my breath. What happened next? He'd marked me. That meant something to shifters. Would we just...run off into the sunset? I grimaced. That didn't seem right. Remy had spoken vows of love and devotion. That was supposed to be normal with mates. I couldn't expect Ovide to love me the same way...

I almost laughed. That didn't seem possible. Nothing did.

Ovide had looked away from me almost instantly, but still, I stared at him. He was just as beautiful as he'd been the night before. Handsome and strong, his essence tugged at me. I decided that when the wedding was over, maybe we should talk. Yeah, I'd corner him. Hell, I wasn't some blushing little flower who had to wait around for a man to approach her and it wasn't like me to be coy and coquettish and bat my eyelashes at a dude to signal I wanted him to make a move.

As soon as the ceremony was over and Remy and Lenni walked back down the aisle together, everyone gathered around them to offer congratulations. But, when the crowd dispersed, and I went to find Ovide, he was gone.

I supposed it was just as well because the feelings that were bubbling to my surface and threatening to break through were scary. They screamed commitment. They screamed forever. I definitely wasn't a forever kind of girl.

"Head's up!" Lenni's voice penetrated my thoughts and reflexively I reached up before I was hit in the face—and caught the bouquet.

Oh, fuck me!

Chapter Ten

MARGO

I supposed it was a good thing I didn't get a chance to talk to Ovide at the wedding yesterday. What would I have said to him anyway? Leave it to me to act like a complete hussy during my first sexual encounter and walk away with a claiming mark. I shoved the thoughts about the parallels to my mother to the back of my mind.

I had been perfectly fine being single. I had never wanted a serious relationship before seeing Ovide. I had so much on my plate, already. The bar was more responsibility than a husband, a child, and a couple of pets all rolled up in one.

I put too much shampoo in my hair and scrubbed my scalp a little too hard as I assessed my current situation. It wasn't fair. How could a one-night-stand change everything so thoroughly? The loss of control of my own emotions was what angered me the most. The guy just shows up and changes my entire life in a matter of a couple of hours?

I knew the truth, though. The real reason it bothered me so much was because I wanted him to want me.

Admitting that to myself wasn't easy. It stung the hell out of my pride. I wanted Ovide and he didn't want me back. I mean, what the fuck was wrong with him? The other dragons hadn't rejected their mates. No way. I could see the way they looked at them. They *loved* their mates, more than I ever thought it was possible to love someone. Maybe a better question was what the fuck was wrong with me?

I hadn't had any kind of representation of romantic love growing up. My mother was a weak and dreamy romantic, my dad was a cold-hearted bastard, and I had been the product of a one-night-stand.

I hadn't even met my dad until, when I was a about eleven, I was able to track him down. He worked for an investment firm in New Orleans. Nance, Lenni and I looked up the bus schedules, mapped out a route to his office, and I paid him a visit.

I'd had all these schoolgirl fantasies of my Dad finding out about me and throwing his arms around me rescuing me from a bipolar mom and a life of poverty. Calling me his princess—Daddy's little girl.

Instead, he told me I was an accident, a huge mistake on his part, and that I shouldn't exist. He said he'd prefer to continue to pretend I didn't exist, and that he did not want to burden his wife by having me around. I would be too much for her to accept.

Looking back, he was no great loss, but I had been devastated at the time. I remember going home, locking myself in my bedroom and then I cried and cried and cried some more. I cried for what seemed like days. And then stopped.

I must have cried out all my tears that day because that was the last time I ever shed another one. My mom and I did okay for a while after that. Then when I was fifteen, she took off. Not even sure where she went, probably followed some guy somewhere, but I was hauled off to foster care.

My first experience witnessing real love had been Lenni and Remy.

But I probably wasn't cut out for anything like they had. Hell, I was faster to fight a guy than I was to flirt with one. I wasn't like other women. Maybe, Ovide could see that.

I finished showering and then got dressed. I was headed back down to the bar to take over for the rest of the night. The Gator Pit was all I needed—my baby, my family, and my biggest and best achievement.

I wasn't expecting to find Nance at the bar when I got there, but I was happy to see her. "You look good on that barstool."

She grinned at me and nodded. "I know."

"What are you doing here?"

"I'm on a date. She's in the bathroom." She shifted. "The wedding yesterday got me all in a romantic mood."

"You could have filled a slop bucket with those tears you shed."

"I'm sentimental, okay? Besides, not everyone's Ms. Stoic like you."

"Are you gonna tell me what you're really doing here?"

She smiled. "Lenni asked me to come check on you."

"And you came with your date?"

Nodding, Nance looked over her shoulder before turning back to me. "I'm supposed to tell you that it'll all work out in the end, but I told Lenni that you would smack me if I repeated that."

"Pretty much."

"So, instead, I'm going to tell you that I'll help you ruin his fucking life if he hurts you."

I laughed. It was refreshing to laugh and I think I shed a layer of angst with Nance's support. "I'll always wish I would've been born gay for you."

A woman appeared at her side and gave me a tight smile. "Hi."

Nance reached across the bar and patted my hand. "You're way too crazy for me. This is...uh...um..."

I bit back a laugh at Nance's look of anguish as she struggled to remember her date's name. "I'm Margo. It's my bar and Nance is my best friend, but it's not my fault that she's so scatterbrained."

"Bev."

The three of us stood there in an awkward silence for a beat until someone raised their empty glass down the bar. I grinned at Nance and winked. "Well, I'm going to get to work. I'm fine. Thanks for checking on me, though."

"You know I can smell a lie, right?" She stood up and took Bev's hand. "When you need me for a little life ruining, just call."

I watched them go. Bev seemed to forgiving Nance's slipup as she shoved her hand in Nance's back pocket. Smiling, I looked down at the bar at the guy waving his glass around. "Put your damn glass down or I'm going to break it over your goddamned head!"

Chapter Eleven

OVIDE

I wanted to see Margo. I was fighting it as hard as I could—the longing, the desire. Foolishly, to take my mind off of the whole mess, I shifted into my dragon thinking it was a good idea to soar through the skies in an attempt to clear my head. Stupid.

My dragon had been itching to get back to Margo, and I no sooner took off in flight than my dragon immediately steered me in the direction of The Gator Pit. I fought it at first, but eventually gave in. I figured she and I needed to talk. Margo had told me the night we met that she wasn't looking for a relationship, but I couldn't help but think I owed her an explanation.

I wanted to check on her, too—make sure she was safe.

I landed behind her bar, but then realized I had nothing to wear. I couldn't exactly enter her establishment without any clothes on. It was like trudging through the fires of hell to convince my dragon to go back home and dress before returning by truck to Margo's bar.

Once I returned, instead of going in, I hung out in the alley near the back door and listened in on what was going on inside as I tried to collect my thoughts and figure out what to say to her. Pure chaos. Shouting, music, shouting over music.

We must have had a connection developing already because I could feel Margo—she was upset and prepared to fight. That stopped all my internal dialogue on a dime and the only thought I had was: *protect Margo.*

I let myself in though the back door, breaking off the door handle in the process. A little thing like a lock wasn't going to keep me from her if she was in danger. Pushing through the packed bar, I saw the cause of the upset. Standing behind a wild, furious looking Margo was a female with a red mark across her face. It looked like a handprint. In front of her, a large human male glared down at Margo.

"What the hell did you think you were doing?" Margo was angry. And I was not exactly sure what the large male had done to earn her ire, but it wasn't hard to guess.

I missed whatever the male said back to her, but I couldn't mistake the sound of even more chaos rising in the bar. People yelled louder. Tension filled the air.

"Get the fuck out!" Margo sounded angrier than ever.

People were yelling at the male, but no one was doing anything to stop the slow movement he made towards Margo. It spurred my dragon into action.

I started shoving people out of my way to get to her, keeping my eyes on her tiny frame. The female behind her cried and cupped her face as the male reached forward, but Margo was ready. Fast as lightning, she snapped her arm forward and shoved her stiffened fingertips into the male's throat. Then, her leg shot forward and the heavy boot she wore connected with his testicles. When he didn't go down instantly, she lifted that lethal foot again and kicked him in the stomach.

I stopped moving, too floored by what I'd just seen. The male stumbled backwards before tripping over someone's foot and going down hard. When he landed, he curled up, reaching for his genitals and the crowd that had gathered around dispersed. The bar went back to its normal level of chaos like nothing had happened.

Margo turned to the female and smiled. "It's going to be okay. He'll be down for long enough for you to get out of here and far away from him. Do you want me to call the cops?"

"I just want to go home."

"That's understandable. But in the morning, I suggest you contact Detective Joe Fuller. He's a good guy. Tell him I witnessed everything." Margo marched slightly ahead of the female, towards the door, clearing a path for her. "You know where I am if you need anything. I'm Margo. I own this bar."

The female smiled hesitantly. "Gina."

I watched as they did an awkward handshake and then Margo stepped away from her. She patted the other female's shoulder and nodded towards the exit. "My number's listed if you need anything at all. He won't hit you again and live to tell the tale."

I moved back through the crowd, towards the back door. Margo was amazing. She was tough and strong. Magnificent.

I wanted to go to her. I was aching to be near her, but it was an ache which I would fight with every ounce of strength in me. I had done enough. There was no need to further complicate her life.

Margo was fine. She did not need a mate. I slipped out of the back door and moved into the shadows intending to return later so I could explain things to her. I owed her an explanation and the sooner the better, but I felt confident about one thing, now. Margo did not need me.

Chapter Twelve

MARGO

Before I realized it, it was almost closing time. Aaron was long gone, since the kitchen only stayed open until ten. I was alone, as usual, but closing was something I could practically do with my eyes closed. There were only a few handfuls of people left nursing their final drinks before having to go home. Two in the morning and we were all tired.

The day had passed in a blur. I was ready to crawl into my bed and sleep. All of my problems would still be there in the morning.

Just when I was telling everyone it was time to leave, the door opened and Ovide strolled in. My body immediately went into a heightened sense of sexual awareness as I watched him sit at the bar and rest his forearms on the old bar top, not meeting my eye.

I walked over to him and sighed. "Last call was five minutes ago. I'm closing."

He looked up, but just watched people leaving. "I know. I just figured I'd make sure everyone left without any trouble."

I bristled in annoyance. "I've been doing this for years, Ovide, all by my little lonesome. I don't need some big, bad dragon protector to look out for lil ol' helpless me."

He finally met my eyes and I saw a flash of gold shoot through his. "I know."

I raised an eyebrow. "Is this some game to get back in my pants? Cause if it is, you can be straightforward. You can get in my pants without pretending to try to protect me. I don't need protecting."

"That is not—"

"I'm not having sex on the floor again, though. Probably." I thought about it, my body still hyper-reacting from him being close again. "Well, maybe..."

"I just wanted to... I wanted..." He didn't seem to know what he wanted and just looked around awkwardly. I was in no mood to help him out, so I just stared at him, adding fuel to his awkwardness. "I will walk you home."

"For sex?"

He grunted. "For safety."

I sighed and rolled my shoulders. "It's not safety I need. I carry a taser and pepper spray and keep a Louisville Slugger behind the bar. Plus, I've never met a man that I wasn't able to bring to his knees with a well-placed foot to the groin. I don't need you for safety."

"Yes, I know. Still—"

"Ovide, sex. Not security. Got it?"

My last customer waved as he stumbled out the door and into a waiting Uber. I rounded the bar heading to the front door to lock it. When I turned back to Ovide, he stood up and backed away. "What happened between us has you scared of me, Ovide? What gives?"

It was his turn to bristle. "I would like to explain about that."

I moved towards him. "Then why are you moving away from me?"

He frowned. "I did not come here to have sex."

I rolled my eyes and went back behind the bar. I needed to finish cleaning the behind the bar area. The rest I could do the next morning. My heart pounded, but I was too tired to get all that worked up over Ovide being weird. "I'll get home just fine. The same way I have for the past, I don't know, decade or two. If that's all you came for, you can leave. I'm good."

He growled. "There are strange males on the street."

"Should I show you how I handle strange males, or are you going to leave me be?"

I could almost feel his annoyance. I didn't care right then, though.

If I wasn't so tired, I would've been more upset about how he was acting.

"I'll wait outside."

I pointed my finger at him. "I'm serious, Ovide. If you aren't walking me home for sex, you aren't walking me home."

He paused and shook his head. "I really just came to talk. What happened between us...it was unusual. It was not normal. I believe it was a mistake."

Suddenly, I was no longer too tired to be angry. "So, now I'm not normal? I'm a mistake? You want to know what's not normal? Sinking your fangs into a woman's neck and then just strolling off into the early morning with nothing to say but 'I'm sorry'. I am not a fucking mistake! You're a fucking mistake!"

He stepped back and frowned. "Like I said, I'll wait outside."

"I swear to god, Ovide, if you're outside this bar when I leave, I will castrate you."

He didn't respond as he left.

I stood there, shaking from anger. Worse, I wasn't just angry at him; I was angry at myself. I'd wanted to have the talk with him about this claiming mark. Instead, when the opportunity arose, he used the word 'mistake' which acted as some sort of bizarre trigger for me and made me explode like an h-bomb. *Way to go, Margo.*

I hurried through closing and locked the bar up. Letting myself out the back, I walked towards my apartment, refusing to look around for Ovide. I meant it when I told him that I could take care of myself. I wasn't some damsel in distress. I left others in fucking distress.

I was a couple feet from my place when Ovide stepped out of the shadows beside me and nearly gave me a heart attack. I swung my bag at him and swore. "What did I say? I said I would castrate you if you were out here!"

"You said the bar."

"What?!"

"You said you would castrate me if I was outside *the bar*. I am not outside the bar."

I counted to ten slowly, trying not to give in and punch his smug mug. "Fine. Okay. Let's talk. I mean, we are mates, right?"

He scowled. "Not exactly."

So much for counting to ten. I was gonna clock him. "You're fucking hilarious."

"What?"

"You're fucking hilarious." I paused. "Did you hear me that time?"

"What are you talking about?"

"I'm talking about the fact that I'm wearing this claiming mark on my neck. You *marked* me. I know enough about shifter shit to know that that's a big deal."

He shook his head and looked away. A heaviness seemed to settle on his shoulders. "Well, it was a mistake, Margo. How many times do I need to say it?"

My chest ached and my throat was dry, but it didn't matter. I wasn't backing down. I needed answers. "A lot more, apparently because I'm just not following."

He growled, but kept his mouth shut. Instead, he moved farther away, closer to the door. His big body was coiled tight.

"This is crazy, Ovide. Why are you doing this? Why are you running and hiding from me?" I sucked in a deep breath and blew it out in a big gush of air. "I just don't get why you're trying to tell me that this mark means nothing."

He came towards me suddenly grasping my upper arms tightly. He leaned down until our faces were level.

"Because I already have a mate!"

Chapter Thirteen

OVIDE

I hated the look of pain on Margo's face. It pierced my chest like a dagger. I'd managed to do what I was pretty sure no one had been able to do before, break through her walls and hurt her. I let go of her arms and backed away. "*Had* a mate."

She rubbed at her arms. "How is that...?"

"I don't fucking know." I rubbed at my face. "Did I hurt you?"

She let out a laugh that held no humor. "Funny question."

"I must go."

"Oh no you don't." She shook her head slowly. "You need to tell me more. You may not be tied to me, but I'm tied to you. I deserve to know the reason that I'll be alone for the rest of my life."

I couldn't. I had already hurt her and the idea of hurting her more by telling her about Kyrian was unacceptable to me. "What else is there to know?"

"Okay, my knowledge of shifters might be limited, but I do know that you can't have two mates. If she was your mate, you wouldn't have slept with me and damned sure wouldn't have marked me. You wouldn't have betrayed her that way. Mates don't... Mates don't do that." Her face crinkled and pain radiated off of her so hard I was almost knocked to my feet. "How is this possible?"

"I don't know!" I ran my hands through my hair and backed farther away from her. I longed to step forward, wrap my arms around her and hold and comfort her. My dragon fought to get free. I couldn't, though. I didn't deserve her and I didn't get a second mate.

"Where is she? Where is your mate?"

I swallowed audibly. "The old world..."

"But when I told you that it was first time having sex. You said it was your first time, too. That was a lie?

"I do not lie."

Somehow, Margo suddenly knew. I could see the moment she understood. Her face collapsed in grief, not for herself. For me. "Oh, Ovide."

"I must go. Now."

"Ovide, wait." She closed the space between us and rested her hand on my arm. The simple touch was too intense, but she didn't withdraw. "How could this happen? Do you think... Do you think that you got a second chance? You couldn't have marked me unless we're mates, too."

"I don't know how it happened. I cannot do it, though, Margo. I cannot move on and act as though Kyrian never happened. It is not right to her and it is not right to you. I cannot be a good mate to you. I cannot give you what you deserve."

Her hand slipped from my arm and the little sound of pain that escaped her mouth would have been from anyone else a tremor, but from her, it was an earthquake. "What do I do?"

I grabbed the door handle, turning away from her. I had to set her free. "You live your life. You find joy and find happiness."

Walking away was a test of resolve and strength because it was the hardest thing I had ever had to do. I know I had hurt Margo, but it had been necessary. It had been the only way to make her understand —to free her.

I took to the sky and fought with my dragon the entire way home. Even once we were home, we fought. He was furious. He knew that Margo was ours. He'd moved on from Kyrian, and wanted Margo to be beside us. I was pissed he could forget Kyrian so quickly. Kyrian deserved more from him. Though, my memory was proving to be weak, as well. Her face was blurrier than ever and I couldn't recall the exact shade of her blonde hair anymore.

None of it mattered, though. I had freed Margo. And myself because I knew what it felt like to bury a mate. Never again.

I found the last bottle of brew that I had from Armand and cracked it open. Not bothering with a glass, I chugged it straight, hoping to numb the pain.

I kept seeing the pained look in Margo's eyes. I doubted her eyes had ever looked that way before. She was a force of nature, taking from life, demanding. An amazing female. Amazing.

I was sorrier than I could admit that she would never be mine.

Chapter Fourteen

MARGO

My gaze was fixed on the B-52's poster on the far wall before it swung to the one with the Beastie Boys next to the dart board. Sara and I had decorated the bar up for the 80's night party I'd decided to host in the hopes of bringing in some added revenue. The place was strewn with posters of 80's bands and movies—Back to the Future, Ferris Bueller's Day Off, The Breakfast Club, Cyndi Lauper, Duran Duran, Eurythmics.

I had spent the entire week in agony and feeling sorry for myself—at work, of course. It wasn't as though I could take the day off and sit around in yoga pants eating ice cream out of the carton and watching game shows. Well, I *was* actually wearing yoga pants. I'd paired them with an off the shoulder, oversized gray sweat shirt with vintage Michael Jackson, Wham, and Frankie Goes to Hollywood buttons that I'd picked up at a thrift store.

Finding out that I wasn't special to Ovide had been hard. He already had a mate. Even though she was long gone, he was still committed to her. Oddly, there was something I found admirable about that—or would have found admirable if it wasn't slowly killing me!

The physical ache was unbearable. I was ready to dry hump the edge of the bar. Lenni had told me there was always an incredibly strong physical pull between mates, but this shit? This shit was too much. I was miserable. My nipples could cut glass, I had to keep a change of underwear in my bag at all times, and I was having perpetual hot flashes. Was this how a cat felt when it went into heat? No wonder they screeched and howled in back alleys.

So far, the night had been a success. We had a packed bar full of 80's costumed customers, Sara was playing DJ and currently blaring Prince's When Dove's Cry. I'd rented a couple big screen TV's and old Atari game consoles and had them hooked up so patrons could play Missile Command and Pac Man. I also borrowed a few Trivial Pursuit board games—80's editions.

The event was a hit, but I was a hot mess. I was using all my damned reserve energy holding myself together, but I couldn't fall apart no matter how much I wanted to. I had a business to run. People depended on me. Drinks didn't pour themselves. Men didn't break up their own drunken brawls. Paychecks didn't sign themselves. It was probably evident to all that I wasn't completely myself. The truth was, I could accept that I would be alone for the rest of my life; it was what I'd always assumed anyway. It was a special kind of torture, though, letting go of Ovide while at the same time knowing that, because of the claiming mark, I would never truly be able to.

For the last few days I'd been avoiding Lenni's calls. She just sounded so...*sad* for me. I couldn't deal with it. I knew Nance was sad for me, but she was fine with drinking and laughing it up, happy to act like nothing was wrong.

Tonight, she was drinking Everclear with a splash of pineapple juice. Her eyes were red and by the slow giggle she was doing, I figured she'd slipped away to smoke some funny stuff at some point.

Probably with the two large bikers she was sitting between. She rested her elbows on the bar and leaned across to me. "You know what? We'll just get married, you and me. I have shit luck with women and you have your thing. We'll just get married and we can have sex once a month—just to relieve tension. I know that you probably won't enjoy it, for multiple reasons, but, hell, it might take the edge off."

Both men's eyes popped out of their skulls, but drunk as skunks themselves, they just laughed. I stopped wiping out the glass I was holding and stared at her. "Huh?"

She laughed. "Okay, fine. No sex."

"And what would I do when you ran around on me?"

"I. Would. Never! You're like the holy grail. Anyone who could walk out on you is a fucking idiot." She winked. "I'm not a fucking idiot."

I just rolled my eyes and filled her glass with straight pineapple juice. "That's debatable. I love you anyway, though."

Another couple of hours passed and Nance had deteriorated into a loose pile of drunk. She was leaning against one of the bikers and they were laughing together about who knew what.

Out of the corner of my eye, I saw the front door open and Lenni walk in. She was dressed in lacy leggings, a bralette, and a miniskirt and loaded down with jelly bracelets, bangles, and neon earrings. Her hair was piled atop her head in a ponytail that was teased to about eight inches tall and loaded down with what was probably and entire can of Aqua Net.

Remi walked in behind her dressed in a white sports coat, white trousers and a black t-shirt, and looked surprisingly like a bigger, buffer, beefier, bearded Don Johnson in his Miami Vice days.

I slipped into the kitchen and started a load of glasses before coming back out and finding Remy, Nance and Lenni all sitting together. The bikers appeared to have vanished.

"You stopped answering my calls." Lenni was upset, I could tell. She even sounded like she was going to cry.

"Don't take it personally. She's avoiding anything related to the D." Nance slurred and fell off the side of her stool. "Ouch."

Lenni wrinkled her forehead. "*Dick?*"

"Dragons."

Remy shot me a look.

"I just...needed some time." I cleared my throat, grabbed a rag and rounded the end of the bar to wash down a couple tables. "What are you two doing out so late? Nice outfits by the way."

Lenni walked down to meet me at the end of the bar and crossed her arms over her chest. "We came to see you. I can't stand this. I can't imagine what you're going through, but I miss you."

I threw the towel down, a little too hard. "Stop it. Stop with the fucking pity party. Every time you look at me, you just look like you're going to cry. I can't forget him when you're looking at me like that!"

To my horror, she did start crying.

"No, Lenni, no. Don't cry." I pulled her into my arms and hugged her. "Don't cry, Lenni. I didn't mean to upset you. I'm sorry. I'm just so on edge lately."

Remy gently pulled her into his arms and blew out a sigh. "This cannot go on forever."

Nance had made it to her feet. "Forever is such a long time for a shifter. They all live for so many fucking years. At least he marked you before deciding he couldn't be with you, Margo. Now, you'll be alive for hundreds of years more."

I stumbled back like one of them had actually shoved me in the chest. "What?"

Nance, not realizing that she'd said anything alarming, continued on while still trying to stay upright. "Yep. Shifters and their mates live forever. Even if you aren't with him."

My gaze shot to Remy, who wasn't denying it, and then Lenni. Their expressions confirmed that what Nance said was true. How did I never know that fact about shifters?

I ran my hands through my hair and tugged at it. Forever? FOREVER? I couldn't even look forward to death in fifty or sixty years to escape the pain?

Forever to feel like my heart was being ripped out and shit on.

Forever to see my friends happily growing old together, having kids and grandchildren and, oh fuck me, great grandchildren!

Forever alone. In agony.

"Margo?"

Everything snapped into place for me. I shook my head. "No. No, this is not going to happen."

Remy cleared his throat. "Margo, what are you thinking? You are making me nervous."

I was thinking that I wasn't going to spend my life being tortured, that's what I was thinking. There had to be a solution. I couldn't go on like that for forever. I was going to have to put away my pride and beg Ovide to either get over his shit and be a real mate to me or put me out of my misery. Sixty years was bad, but forever? No fucking way. I wouldn't do it.

"Where is Ovide's house?"

Remy shuddered. "What are you thinking?"

"I'm thinking of giving him one chance—one last chance. He can agree to a mating—a real mating, or he can end me. His choice. If he doesn't want me, that's fine, but I'm not living forever like this."

Lenni looked horrified. "What?! Margo, no! What are you talking about?"

I went behind the bar and grabbed Nance's car keys which I'd confiscated earlier in the evening. "I'm talking about making something happen. It's now or never. I'm sick of sitting around being sad and mopey. I'm sick of hurting and feeling like someone is stabbing me in the heart with every thought I have of him. Which, by the way, is A LOT. I'm sick of it all."

It wasn't like me to sit back and wait on something once I'd made a decision. And I had made a decision. For whatever reason, before that moment, I'd just accepted the whole sordid mess. No more, though. It was time for action.

None of this achiness, this fevered longing, was going to go away. It wasn't going to fade with more time passing like I'd hoped.

It would continue—FOREVER!

Oh, fuck me.

Chapter Fifteen
OVIDE

I flew over the wall surrounding Magnolia Plantation, Angel's ancestral home, and landed on the manicured lawn before shifting. I had been summoned by Armand, a summons I would normally have ignored, but this one was at the request of his mate. I was fond of Angel. She and I shared an understanding of the darkness I harbored inside; one that came as a result of deep loss and sorrow.

I had no idea what she wished to speak to me about.

Yes, I did. I had a very good idea. It was about the claiming mark. The horrible, shameful mistake I made which I would forever regret.

I strolled across the rolling grounds of the estate glancing out at the sparkling lake beyond. It was a picture of tranquility with the reflected sunlight sparkling off its surface. As I climbed the stairs to the front door, it opened before I knocked. Armand had anticipated my arrival.

Armand merely nodded in greeting. I nodded back. "Hello brother.'

He handed me a fluffy pink bathrobe to cover myself. "Angel told me to give you this to wear."

While dragons had no modesty, and nudity in our human form was as natural to us as nudity in our beast form, humans thought otherwise. As such, the dragon males had grown so that they did not like other males naked in front of their mates.

I shrugged into the bathrobe. I had worn the garment before. It was of excellent quality and I adored it. "Angel wishes to speak to me?"

"We both do. I would like to ask if you have taken leave of your senses. My mate, however, has more sympathy that I have. What have you done?"

I sighed. "I can't explain what I don't understand."

"So, you did mark her?" Angel was descending the marble stairs and I met her questioning gaze. "She *is* your mate? But, you said..."

"I know. It should not work this way." I shook my head, frustrated. "It just happened. Everything just happened. I did not mean to. I did not want to." Well, that wasn't entirely true. I had wanted to mark her at the time. Very much so. "She is not my mate. She cannot be."

"What are the two of you talking about?" Armand scowled and crossed his arms over his chest.

"I haven't told Armand anything about, uh, you know what—your *past*. I wanted your permission first."

I paused for a moment, and then nodded.

Angel turned to her mate and placed her hand on his arm. "Babe, Ovide already had a mate. Back in your old world."

Armand's eyes widened so much it looked as though his eyeballs would fall out of his head. "Wh-Where? W-Why? That cannot be. How can that be?"

Both turned their gazes on me. Armand's, stunned; Angel's, sympathetic. I wanted to explain, but I was unable to form the words. The air would not travel from my lungs through my throat and over my tongue.

Finally, Angel spoke up. "She died."

Armand stumbled backwards, his arms flailing behind him looking for purchase, which he found. He grasped onto the arms of an antique, stuffed chair and dropped into it before running his fingers through his hair looking as though he'd just heard news so shocking it was difficult to comprehend—which I supposed he had. "No. That cannot be true." He looked up at me, clearly expecting a response. "It cannot be true."

"I do not lie."

Angel and I stared at him for several minutes until Angel spoke, "Babe? Are you okay?"

Armand cleared his throat before he spoke, and when he did, his voice held a tone which I despised. One which served as the sole reason I had kept Kyrian a secret from the others—pity.

"Why have you never spoken of it, brother?" But as his eyes met mine, he knew. He understood that I did not want to feel the pity of others. And he quickly masked his emotions. His forehead wrinkled in thought. "How is it you were able to claim another?"

"I do not know that. But I am deeply ashamed to have marked another."

Armand looked over at his mate. I had no doubt he understood my shame at that moment.

"Hold on here a minute." Angel's fists were digging into her hips and a scowl lined her face. "There is nothing to be ashamed of!"

Her look was so adamant that I was completely shocked. "How can you say that? I have forsaken Kyrian."

"You haven't forsaken her! She died. Big difference."

Armand stood. "I must agree with my mate." He slid his arm around Angel's shoulder and gazed down at her as though she was his reason for being. Pain struck me like a blow to the gut. "Fate knows what it's doing. If another mate has been provided for you, you should accept gratefully."

"Exactly!" Just then a small device attached to Angel's hip began crying like a youngling. "Baby monitor. Mia's up. Hold that thought. I'll be right back."

As Angel scurried back up the stairs, Armand ushered me into a sitting room. "You never told anyone," he mumbled. Then he took a deep breath. "Brother, I do not pretend to know everything about how fated mates work. I only know that the pairings do work."

A part of me wanted to believe him—longed to have with another what he and Angel clearly shared. No, not just with another—with Margo.

"Armand is right." Angel entered the room holding Mia who was cooing and clinging tightly with slobbery fists to her mother's hair. "You don't have to lose the memory of your past love to move on to another. That's the beautiful thing about love—it's unlimited. You never run out. Hearts expand. But what you're doing now is not forsaking Kyrian. It's dissing Margo. And she deserves better."

Armand looked as though he was still digesting the shock of the news he had just received. "All this time you have been in mourning?"

"All this time I have felt as though a part of me was missing. Hollow." Until Margo.

Armand looked at me thoughtfully for several seconds while Angel extracted a clump of her hair from the slobbery little fist and replaced it with a small toy.

"I have a question for you, brother." Of course he had. He probably had a hundred questions. I wasn't sure I would be able to answer any of them, though. I shot him a look which didn't deter him from voicing his query.

"What was she like?"

His question puzzled me. "What was..."

"Your mate...Kyrian. What was she like?"

"Well, she was soft-spoken, gentle, delicate." Her delicateness was perhaps one of the reasons she came down with the illness she did. It was highly uncommon for a dragon to get sick, but not impossible. We had our share of diseases and ailments to which we were susceptible, but it was rare to even know someone who had contracted one, and even rarer to know someone who had died from one. "She was truly the gentlest, fairest dragoness in the land."

Angel and Armand shared a conspiratorial look which I didn't understand.

When Mia became squirmy, Angel handed her off to Armand who smiled at the youngling as though she was his world. "Ovide, forgive me for saying this, but I can't imagine you mated to someone who was delicate and gentle."

I snorted. "I was a different dragon then. Young, naive, unjaded."

Angel nodded. "And now you aren't."

Armand barked a laugh. "Now he is cranky, sour and difficult."

"Not too many women can handle a guy like that. Sounds to me as though Kyrian was perfect for the young Ovide, but since her death, you have grown and changed. You're not the same person you once were. I mean if you met a woman like Kyrian today, I would guess the two of you might be incredibly mismatched. Yet..."

Yet, Margo was perfect. Exactly the type of female who was not intimidated by me or my personality. She was bold and brash herself— a quality that I admired. The corner of my mouth turned up in a half-grin as I thought about Margo's barbed tongue. Stimulating, refreshing, exhilarating. No, Margo and Kyrian were nothing alike. I must have been silent for a long time because I was almost startled out of my reverie by Angel.

"Margo's a badass, yeah. She's tough. But no one is tough enough not to hurt when rejected. She doesn't deserve that. And, just because you love again does not mean you have to erase the memory of what you shared with Kyrian. It's possible to have two great loves."

Was it? And, was I really hurting Margo? I couldn't pretend to understand how the entire situation occurred. It seemed to defy nature. Perhaps because Kyrian and I never actually physically mated, because there had been no claiming mark, I was granted another mate. I could think of no other explanation, but did I really need an explanation? I hated the thought of Margo in pain and hated even more that I might be the cause of it.

I got up to leave. "I will think hard about it." It was all I could promise. But, for the first time in over a century, my heart felt light and...hopeful.

Chapter Sixteen
MARGO

My final decision: fuck this!

I wasn't going to live for eternity—or who the hell knew how long—with an ache in my gut and the sting of rejection hovering over me constantly. I was going to find Ovide's dragon ass, confront him and demand he step up and start taking this mating crap seriously, or he could just put a bullet in my head.

Or I'd jump off a cliff.

Maybe run my car in to a brick wall.

Whatever. Point was, if he refused to be the yang to my yin, then I'd be checking out of this cold, cruel world of my own volition and on my own terms. Fate would not be dicking me around.

I got the general idea of where Ovide lived from Remy and headed that way, my foot heavy on the gas pedal. I'd seen the other dragons' houses. Dragon homes were basically huge structures—castles they called them—so I had a feeling it would be hard to miss Ovide's.

I took Nance's car—she was in no condition to drive anyway—and headed to where I thought it was.

Later, I was able to admit that all of it, from A to Z, was a bad plan. I should've slept on it and re-examined my impulsive agenda in the morning, but I had just been pushed too far that night. Anxiety like I'd never known spurred me on, the idea of spending forever alone was a concept I couldn't even begin to digest.

I drove to the small town of Ferrer's Corner following the directions that Remy had given me. Unfortunately, he gave directions from an overhead viewpoint, not an on-the-ground view. When I got near, I realized that there was no way to travel by car from the main road in town to my destination which was a mile deep in a forest.

I was far too incensed to let a little thing like trees deter me, though. I parked at the side of the road and marched into the densely packed woods.

After walking through the woods for what felt like hours, with only the flashlight from my cell phone to light the way, I started realizing that my plan had been incredibly stupid. It was too late to turn back, though. I'd been walking for too long. The way back had to be much farther than the way ahead. I kept going straight, thinking that I would come to the clearing with a house eventually. At least I thought I was going straight. Wasn't I?

If anything, the woods got thicker.

It was pitch dark in the middle of the trees. The thick canopy of branches blocked any moonlight from penetrating. My phone barely seemed adequate. Besides the occasional sound of an owl in the distance, everything was silent. My clumsy footfalls were the only things that could be heard in the overwhelming clusters of trees.

I managed to stay calm, relative term in my current situation, for a while. When my phone beeped to tell me that it was going dead, my biggest fear turned from spending forever alone and achy to being lost in the middle of the woods with nothing but a dead phone and my imagination to keep me company.

In my panicked state, I decided it would be better to turn around and go back to the car, so I did just that. Only, everything looked the same. In the inadequate light of a cell phone, every fallen branch and tree trunk looked like the next.

Getting truly desperate, I dialed Lenni's number, but I'd waited too long. The beep of the phone telling me that the call couldn't connect pushed me over the edge I'd been teetering on for weeks.

Run, Margo, run.

It was the only answer. I knew it was only a matter of time before I was left without a shred of illumination and I needed to get out of the woods before that happened. I'd seen too many Dateline NBC episodes to think I would be safe all alone out there. The light of my phone shook violently as I leapt over and around fallen logs and branches and jogged in the direction I thought the car was.

I knew I was fucked the moment the light captured a set of glowing eyes ahead of me, low to the ground. The vicious snarl would've been hard to miss. I froze where I was and tried to run through any knowledge my brain had filed away on wild dogs in the woods.

Nothing. I had nothing.

Ears straight back, the dog slowly slunk towards me. Hoping it was just someone's pet that had gotten out and just wanted to sniff my hand and get a scratch behind the ears, I held my breath as it approached.

When it was closer, however, I realized letting it sniff my hand was a bad idea and trying to scratch behind its ears was an even worse idea. It was not somebody's pet dog that had gotten out of the gate. Nope, this guy was not a pet.

It was a wolf.

Just as it opened its mouth and lunged towards me, I swung my arm down and hit it on the top of the head with my phone. Hard enough to splinter pain through my hand and halfway up my arm, it didn't deter the wolf for more than a second.

As its teeth clamped down on my leg, I felt a snap under the wolf's dangerously powerful jaw. I screamed a blood curdling scream and pounded at the animal with my fists as pain tore through my limb.

Writhing on the ground, I fought for my life. I found a small, fallen branch beside me and used it to fight the beast off. Screaming at it with everything I had left in me, I wailed on it with the makeshift club. I got in a couple really good whacks, too.

It must've decided I wasn't worth the trouble. Snarling at me once more, it turned and sauntered off.

I dragged myself to a tree and rested my back against it while trying to examine my leg. I couldn't see it, though. I couldn't see a thing. I'd dropped my phone and I was in complete darkness. Fear crept up my spine and into my throat as I realized that wolves usually travelled in packs. What if he came back with the rest of his pack-mates to finish me off? No way I could fight them off. I wouldn't even see their approach. Feeling around me wildly, I searched for another branch to protect myself with.

Something crawled across my hand and I cried out again. I was going to die in the woods. No one would find my body. The wolf would finish me off—pick my bones clean— and I'd just be a memory. Not even a fond memory to most.

I trembled in fear and pain while dragging a branch closer and then I ripped off my shirt and used it to wrap around my leg as a bandage. The pain was excruciating. Worse, I could feel the blood soak through my shirt before I even got it tied all the way. I was probably going to bleed to death.

I didn't want to die. I wasn't ready. The irony wasn't lost on me. Just hours earlier, I'd wanted to face off with Ovide and demand he mate me or end my life. And there I was—at death's door.

Anger flooded my body as I thought about dying in the woods while trying to beg my mate to accept me. What the fuck had I been thinking? How humiliating. Thank god, it never got as far as the begging stage. I'd rather die fighting than rejected and begging.

I knew full well I might die. I also knew I was a fighter. I gritted my teeth and dug my back into the bark of the tree. I wasn't going out just sitting there bleeding.

I took off my bra and used it as a tourniquet to tie off my leg above my knee. I screamed from the pain, but it was good. Pain meant that I wasn't dead. I knew I couldn't walk on the leg, but I could crawl.

I didn't know where I was crawling to, but I slowly moved to my stomach and managed to dig the knee of my good leg into the packed earth and with my hands progress a couple feet forward. My chest and stomach dragged the ground and sticks ripped at my skin, but I kept going. My leg throbbed and I grew weak and dizzy, but I still kept going.

I was not going out on my knees, begging a man to accept me.

"Margo!"

My heart pounded. I thought I heard Ovide's voice. Fuck, I was hearing things. That wasn't a good sign. I tried to pull myself across the forest floor faster. If I could get to the car, maybe I could honk until someone came. At the very least, I could lock myself in.

The ground shook around me with footsteps. The wolf was back. My fingers brushed against a branch and I flung myself over, ready to fight for my life. Screaming like a wild woman, I swung the branch with everything in me. Fuck that furry asshole.

"Margo!" Ovide's voice again. Maybe it wasn't an auditory hallucination. If it was, then the wolf was definitely going to win.

"Hang on. Hang on, Margo."

I felt myself being lifted and gasped at the pain. I opened my eyes and saw nothing. I felt Ovide, though. I sensed it was his arms holding me and I let my head fall back.

I managed to croak out what I figured would be my very last words. "I didn't die begging for you. I fought."

Chapter Seventeen

OVIDE

I sat in the waiting room of a human hospital for the first time in my life. It was a wretched place that smelled of sickness, death, and disinfectant. And blood. Margo's blood. Or perhaps that was me. I was covered in Margo's blood. They'd mopped it up from the floor already where it had dripped in puddles.

I didn't die begging for you. I fought. Her last words to me ricocheted around my head. I knew what she meant. After Remy asked me if Margo had made it, he'd told me that she'd been coming to demand that I take her as my mate or she would end her life.

I knew she wouldn't really do it. That female didn't have an ounce of "give up" in her. But that wasn't the point. The point was that I had failed her miserably. Angel was right, I had rejected her. I hadn't thought of it that way at the time, but it was exactly what I had done.

Images of her on her back, covered in dirt and blood, hollering and swinging a branch nearly her size—fighting like a true warrior—remained ingrained in my psyche.

I hadn't expected to find her like that. I'd heard her scream, and, through the mate bond, I'd felt her fear and her resolve. I'd gone out to find her right away. Even when I'd smelled the blood, I had no idea it would be so bad.

I hung my head and tried to hold myself together. No matter what I told myself, I could not stop thinking that Margo was somewhere in this hospital, dying. They wouldn't let me go back with her. They'd called security and threatened to have me arrested if I didn't stop shouting demands and threatening staff. I calmed for the moment, fully intending to sneak back when they were not observing me. They did not understand. I needed to be near her. I needed to assure myself that she was okay.

I had to tell the others. Lennox would want to know. I could not clear my mind enough to open the line of communication with my brothers, though. I could not focus in such a heightened state.

All I could think about was Margo fighting for her life, clinging to her life—hearing her say that she would not die begging. Proud, even in what could have been her demise, she was stronger than any warrior I'd ever known.

"Sir?"

I looked up and then jumped to me feet when a human male in a white coat came towards me. "How is she?"

"She's going to be okay. She has to have surgery on that leg to repair the bone, but she's a tough cookie. We'll give her more blood to stabilize her, but after that and the surgery, I expect her to make a full recovery." He looked away and smiled. "I've never seen someone come in like that and still manage to blacken a nurse's eye while trying to free herself."

All the blood drained from my head and I sank into the chair. Too small for my large body, it creaked its objection. She would not die.

"Surgery can be a tricky thing sometimes, so I rarely make promises. But, sometimes the prognosis is based more on the attitude of the patient than on the injury. That lady's a fighter. I'd lay a wager that your girlfriend is going to be just fine."

I just nodded at him.

"We're going into surgery in an hour. Do you want to see her before then? She's heavily medicated, but she's been coming in and out."

"Yes." I stood up and followed him out of the waiting room and down a long hallway. When he gestured for me to go into a room to my left, I grew anxious.

"Go on in. You can sit with her until she's ready to go back."

I was suddenly transported in my mind back over a century ago, to when I was a younger dragon, distraught, heartbroken, lingering beside Kyrian's deathbed. I was terrified to see how bad Margo was, scared that it was all a joke and she was already dead. It was the low groan from inside the room that finally snapped me out of my head and yanked me forward.

The bed made her look even smaller than she was. Margo had been cleaned up. A gown covered her naked chest, but I could still see small scratches on her arms and above the collar of the hospital gown. Her face had a few, too. Covered in several blankets, she was hooked to machines and the constant beeping from them added to the foreboding atmosphere.

I sank into the chair next to her bed and stared at her. Such a contradiction. So delicate of form and fierce of spirit. She'd nearly died. My fault. All my fault. I should have been by her side. Caring for her, protecting her, trying to be the mate to her that she deserved. My mate, left to bleed out on the forest floor while trying to get me to give her a chance. What had I done?

"Fucker."

I snapped my eyes up to Margo's face and found her hazy eyes trying to focus on mine. I knelt next to her and leaned into her. "Yes, I'm here."

Her eyes rolled in her head but she managed to focus on me again. "I think I scratched my nipples off."

I quickly shook my head. "I checked."

She scowled and then her eyes rolled back again. I was spared a verbal lashing by whatever medication she was on.

I stayed where I was, leaning over her, staring at her, incredibly grateful that she was still alive. I'd been given a second chance with a mate and I'd almost let her slip through my fingers.

A commotion in the hallway caught my attention. Just as I was standing up to make sure Margo was safe, the door opened and Lennox stumbled in. Her eyes red and swollen from crying, she spotted Margo and sobbed. Remy was right behind her, also visibly shaken.

"What are you...? How'd you know...?"

Remy clasped my arm. "You've been screaming into all of our heads since you found her."

Lennox held Margo's hand and cried openly. "Oh, Margo, I'm so sorry. We should never have let you go. I'm so, so sorry."

"The others are out in the waiting room. We weren't supposed to be allowed back, but Lennox cried at someone until they gave in." He moved over to his mate's side to comfort her. "Your mate is quite the warrior."

I stood on her other side of the bed and balled my fists at my sides. I wanted to hold Margo's hand in mine, but I didn't deserve to. "I was going to wait until the morning to contact you."

Lennox glared at me. "I'm glad your brain had more sense than you did."

Remy rubbed her neck and sighed. "I understand, brother, but we should be here with you."

I was glad they were. For whatever reason, knowing my brethren were nearby helped me to feel slightly calmer. I'd been closing myself off from everyone for so long, I didn't know what it was like to really rely on them as though they were—family.

"What attacked her?" Lennox wiped her eyes and choked back another sob.

"A wolf."

Remy swore. "I shouldn't have let her go."

"It's not your fault." I ran my hands through my hair. "It's my fault."

"You're damn right, it is." Lennox glared at me through her red, swollen eyes. "You don't deserve her."

I sank back into the chair next to Margo. "Tell me something I don't know."

Chapter Eighteen

MARGO

I wasn't sure what was happening when I woke up. My body didn't feel like my own and I could hear people talking over me. I couldn't remember where I was or why there would be people around while I was sleeping. I tried to shift into a more comfortable position and sharp pain shot through my body.

Grunting, I opened my eyes and blinked. I needed ibuprofen.

"She's awake!"

I looked around and tried to reach up to rub at the grit and grime blocking my vision. It didn't take me long to realize I was hooked to something that hurt when I pulled at it.

"Margo, sweetie?" Lenni's voice floated into my ear. "Don't pull at your IV, honey."

IV? I reached up with my other hand and rubbed my eyes. Blinking rapidly, I looked around in shock. A room full of people stared at me. "What the fuck is going on?"

Someone moved beside the head of the bed. I turned my head to find Ovide looking down at me. He wore a faint smile as he held a cup of water out to me. "Hey."

I was dead.

Had to be.

I fought to sit up, knocked into his hand and splashed some of the water in my face.

And, I was in hell.

"Hey, Margo, it's okay. You're in the hospital. Do you remember what happened?"

I looked back at Ovide, unable to stop my traitorous eyes from straying that way. He was so beautiful. Standing there, looking uncomfortable, his hang-dog eyes...puppy dog eyes...big, bad wolf eyes... WOLF!

I gasped aloud as my brain snapped into place and everything came rushing back in an instant. My hands grasped at the blankets over me, I needed to see my leg. I couldn't feel it. Holy shit, I couldn't feel my leg! Was it even still there? Did I have a leg?

"You're okay, Margo. You're okay, I promise." Lenni helped me uncover my leg and showed me the cast it was in. "You had to have surgery on your leg to fix it. You're okay, though."

I sank back into the bed and breathed a sigh of relief.

"You fought off a wolf, single-handedly. That is some special magic right there, little witch." Remy moved over next to Lenni and smiled down at me.

This was too much. All of it. I was overwhelmed and freaked out. My body hurt and if I possessed the ability to cry, I probably would have. I was in a nightmare of my least-finest extended moment. And I had an audience. Lovely. "I just need...a few minutes alone. Please."

"Of course. We'll come back a little later, okay?" Lenni kissed the top of my head and backed away. "I love you."

They filed out. When I was alone, I buried my face in my hands and groaned. I couldn't believe I'd survived. It had been pretty iffy out there. In fact, I'd been sure I was about to meet my maker. I just refused to go down without a fight. Which showed how stupid I'd been thinking I was going to give Ovide an ultimatum. Be my mate, or kill me now. Dumb.

Actually, the only reason I hadn't been mauled to death by that wolf was because of Ovide. I could lie to myself and say he was the reason I'd been there in the first place, but I knew the truth. It was my own fault for going into the forest that late. The idea of forever without Ovide hadn't been something I could swallow. Death had seemed better, until I was face to face with it.

"You scared me."

I jumped and let out a scream, not realizing that Ovide was still standing slightly behind me. I tried to twist to face him, but it hurt too much. "What the fuck are you doing here? I thought you'd left."

He moved around so he was in front of me. "No. I am not leaving."

A nurse picked that moment to waltz in. She sported a nasty shiner, but she looked happy to see me up. "Hey, Sugar Ray! Someone out there mentioned that you were awake and I wanted to come in and check on you. How are you feeling?"

"Like wolf chow."

She pointed to her eye. "You've got a killer right hook."

I gaped at her. "You're kidding?"

She laughed easily, obviously not holding a grudge. "Nope. You ever give up wolf wrangling, you'd have quite a career ahead of you in the boxing ring." She scanned the monitors and checked my IV. "I'll order you more medicine, okay? Do you want anything else? You're not on a restrictive diet or anything, so I can get you whatever you want, when you're ready."

I glanced over at Ovide. I wasn't hungry. I just felt sick to my stomach. Looking back at her, I shook my head. "I'm good."

She left and Lenni popped her head back in the door. "You need to eat. I'll send Remy to smuggle you in some take out."

"I'm not hungry."

"I'll send him anyway."

When she was gone and the door was shut again, Ovide sighed. "You should eat. You lost a lot of blood last night."

I shook my head. I felt humiliated. What a screw up. No wonder he didn't want me.

"Are you hurting?" He moved closer. "Can I do anything?"

I stared up at the ceiling and shook my head. "I'm fine."

"Come on, Margo, you—"

"Why are you here, Ovide?" I growled as I grew more goddamned frustrated by the second. "Why are you here? You don't want to be, and you don't have to be, so why don't you fucking leave?"

"I do want to be here."

"So, what, since I'm in the hospital you suddenly feel the need to play the good mate? I'm fine. I'm not dying. Thanks for saving me, but you don't owe me anything else. I don't need your pity and I sure as hell don't need you to play nursemaid. Go home."

He closed the distance between us and sat in the chair next to me. "I will not leave."

"Dammit, Ovide, go home!"

The door opened again and Lenni stuck her head back in. "Everything okay in here?"

"Get out!" Ovide barked the order out with a barely constrained anger in his voice. "Give us at least five minutes alone."

To her credit, Lenni ignored him entirely and directed her focus on me. "You okay?"

I nodded. "I'm fine, Lenni. Thanks for checking."

As soon as she'd closed the door again, Ovide leaned in toward me. "I am not leaving. I deserve whatever ire and harsh words you have for me, so go ahead, I am listening. But I promise you right now, anyone who tries to make me leave this room will NOT succeed."

I looked away from him, at the small TV hanging from the ceiling. It wasn't on, and I could see a teeny tiny reflection of us in the darkened screen. "Fine. Do whatever you want."

"I am."

"Great."

"Great."

The nurse came back in with a syringe and smiled, seemingly oblivious to the tension in the room. "Okay. Here come the happy drugs. This will knock out any pain you're feeling."

"Will it knock me out, too?"

She grinned. "Without a doubt."

"Thank god for that." I leaned back in the bed and closed my eyes, waiting for it to hit. Maybe when I woke up again, everything would be back to normal. That's what I wanted, right?

A light pressure from Ovide resting his hand on the bed beside mine drew my eyes to the sight. His finger inched towards mine and then stopped. I looked up and found him watching me.

I was just about to say something—not sure what—when a wave of drowsiness swept me into lala land.

That was all I remembered.

Chapter Nineteen

MARGO

The moment I could get up and walk, I was kicking all their asses. I was furious with the dragon gang and even more so with my two besties. Beyond furious.

"You might as well stop mean-mugging us. It's the only option." Nance shrugged and fussily draped a blanket over me. I shrugged it off angrily and continued to glower. "Besides, everyone is in agreement that this is the best thing for you."

I wanted to punch someone. Instead of taking me home like I'd thought they were doing, they pulled a bait and switch and carted me off to the middle of nowhere—or should I say to Ovide's home out in the middle of nowhere. And they were seriously going to leave me there. With Ovide. In his home.

There I was sprawled out on the couch, half doped up with pain meds, without a single escape route in sight. There was no way to scram if things got awkward. Which of course they always did between Ovide and me. I felt like a caged animal. Trapped. Shoot me now.

I threw my hands in the air dramatically and rolled my eyes to the ceiling. "Best thing for me? No one is thinking about me, or my feelings! The best thing for me is not spending the next few weeks stuck in close proximity to a man who'd rather I didn't exist."

As if on cue, Ovide walked in with Remy. He glanced at me, scowling, then looked away. Ha! Proof that he was as horrified by the situation as I was. Who the hell talked him into this? And what had they done to get him to agree to it? Threats? Bribery? Coercion?

Lenni squeezed my hand. "I love you. You know that. We're all taking shifts at the bar while you recover. Cezar and Cherry are there now and Remy and I will relieve them at six."

Remy wrapped his arm around his mate puling her against his side. "Do not worry about your bar, little witch, we will handle things at The Gator Pit."

"Nance and I will be over to check on you all the time. It's not forever. You just need to be somewhere safe while you heal. Ovide will take care of you and make sure you're not walking on that leg sooner than you're supposed to." Lenni gestured to Ovide who was standing with his arms crossed over his chest, stern faced and wearing that damned scowl.

I lowered my voice. "I'm sure Ovide's tickled pink about that. What, did he draw the short straw?"

"No, silly. He volunteered. Well, actually, volunteered isn't the right word. Insisted."

"He did not."

"Mmm-hmm. I think his exact words included something about never letting you out of his sight again."

I huffed a sigh of disbelief. Nice try, Lennox, but I'd believe that B.S. right after I saw pigs with wings and Hell's popsicles. I stewed quietly, torn between wanting to kick my conniving, lying friends out the door and wanting to lasso them to a chair so they wouldn't leave. There was not much else I could do. I had no one else to help me out.

While Lenni plugged a phone charger in and Nance unpacked the snacks and bottled water they'd brought for me, I pondered whether there was some kind of super-vitamin I could take that would speed up my healing and knit my broken bones together faster. The surgeon had said no walking for a month which meant a month of needing assistance dressing, going to the bathroom...not to mention showering. Oh, fuck me.

Why had I ever thought it was a good idea to confront Ovide? I should have just accepted my fate and learned to live with being an estranged mate, a.k.a. loser reject? But no, instead I had to go traipsing off in the woods half-cocked and ending up sentencing myself to month of infirmity in the presence of the very man who had rejected me.

"Okay, Nance and I will be back tomorrow. We'll make an appointment with the orthopedic surgeon next week, and a physical therapist will be coming the following Friday to discuss the program for rebuilding your strength. A nurse will come by once a week to check on you." Lenni ticked items off on her fingers, even though she'd already gone over everything multiple times. "We're off for now. I'm sure you're tired and could use a nap."

"I'll bring a TV over tomorrow." Nance leaned in closer. "What kind of guy doesn't own a TV?" She shifted her narrowed eyes to Ovide and studied him skeptically for a second. "That's suspect in my book."

"If Ovide angers you, use your magic on him." Remy patted my head again like I was a favorite pet. When I snapped my teeth at him, he backed away, hands raised, wearing a stupid ass grin. I was beginning to think he just liked to fuck with me.

I frowned. "You do realize that I'm not a dog, right?"

He just laughed.

Lenni wrapped her arm around him and gave me an apologetic look. "You'll be back on your feet in no time."

I could feel Ovide eyeballing me. I didn't think I was ready to be alone with him. I felt panicky at the prospect.

"Are you sure you can handle the bar? Because I can go over some basics with you." I should've been embarrassed at how desperate I was to keep them in the room with me. "It's not easy."

Nance wasn't having any of it, though. "We got it covered. Lord knows, I've been on the other side enough times to know what goes on." Nance slowly backed away and pulled Lenni with her. "Alright, have fun! You two don't do anything I wouldn't do!"

"Don't try to do too much, Margo. Let Ovide help you."

Remy snorted. "Don't turn him into a newt, okay?"

I scowled as I watched them leave. Ovide walked out with them and I was alone in his living room for the first time. The place was adorable—a small log cabin, clean and tidy, and very sparsely decorated. Not at all what I had expected. The other dragons had huge, big old drafty homes—castles, whatever—that were way too ostentatious for my taste. Ovide's place was homey. I was settled on the couch, and from there I could see a couple easy chairs surrounding the couch, a kitchen table with four chairs, and a large fireplace.

With my phone gripped in one hand, useless, since I couldn't get a single bar of service, and a bottle of water in the other hand, I wished I did have magical powers. I would've turned myself into a house fly so I could buzz the hell out of there.

My emotions were all over the place and it seemed that Ovide was experiencing that same struggle. He'd been nice, but distant. He would stare at me with a mixture of what I interpreted as anger, sadness, and guilt on his face when he didn't think I could see him. I felt like I'd trapped him.

Yet another reason to be ashamed. What I'd done had been so stupid. I'd driven out to the middle of nowhere and stomped through the woods like a mad woman to demand that he stop playing the avoidance game and treat me like a true mate—or what? Kill me? Brilliant. *Next endeavor, rocket science... Margo, you genius you.*

The only sliver of sunshine in the whole mess was that I'd learned something from all of it. I'd learned that the only thing worse than having your mate reject you was having them reject you and then feel obligated remain at your side.

Ovide didn't want to play nursemaid any more than I wanted to be stuck in this tiny cabin with a gimp leg. Despite what Lenni said about him insisting I stay with him, I was sure that the gang had forced him into taking care of me. Lenni probably put pressure on Remy who put pressure on Ovide.

So, not only was I a hostage, I was a hostage to a hostile caregiver.

I dropped my head back on the arm of the couch and groaned. At least his furniture was comfortable.

"Are you in pain? Do you need more medicine?"

I jumped as the sound of Ovide's voice broke through the silence, but kept my gaze on the ceiling. It was a lovely vaulted ceiling with exposed log beams that crisscrossed. "No. I'm okay."

Eyes still on the ceiling, I heard him sit in the chair beside me. And then nothing. He was completely silent, to a point that I didn't even know if he was breathing. I was too uncomfortable to look, but I listened hard. I didn't hear anything.

When I held my breath to see if I could hear him, he finally spoke. "What are you doing?"

"What? Nothing."

"Why are you holding your breath?"

"I'm not."

"You were."

"No, I wasn't."

"I heard you."

"How could you hear me if I wasn't breathing?"

He sighed. "Do you need anything?"

I finally turned my head to look at him and realized that he didn't look so good. With dark bags under his eyes and exhaustion clear in the downward turn of his mouth, I felt myself soften towards him. He didn't appreciate this situation any more than I did. "A nap, I guess."

"I will carry you to the bed. You will be more comfortable."

I shook my head emphatically. "No, no. I'm good here."

"It is not a problem. I will carry you, Margo."

The way he said my name—with a slight roll of the "r" sent tingles through my sore body and made me think of what else he could do with that tongue and how good he was at it. That, if nothing else, made me hold my hand up to adamantly stop his approach. "I said I'm good here! Do not touch me!"

He sank back in the chair and frowned. "I will have to touch you eventually. If you have not noticed, you cannot move yourself."

"You'll touch me only when absolutely necessary. No unnecessary touching. Neither of us asked for this and I'm sorry that I was thrust on you this way, but we're just going to have to deal with it. Touching as little as possible will help. Probably."

He looked...something. Sad, maybe? He stood up and turned towards the kitchen. He took a few steps and then stopped. "I did ask for this. I do want you here."

I stared at his back, frozen in disbelief. Did he just say what I thought he did or was that the pain meds hearing things funny? Pretty sure he said he wanted me here, but it had to be a sense of obligation making him say it. Didn't it?

"Why?"

Ovide turned, a brow raised questioningly.

"I just want to know why you want me here. And I want the truth."

"I do not lie."

"It's because you felt guilted into it when the others asked you, isn't it?"

"No. It is not. The others did not ask. I demanded."

I narrowed my eyes and studied him. "Again, *why?*"

He appeared flustered for a moment. "Because...you are my mate I should be caring for you. It makes sense—"

"Because you feel guilty. As though this was somehow your fault."

"I do feel guilty, but that is not why I insisted. It is for a far more selfish reason." His dark eyes burned into me, his perpetual scowl still present.

"Again, why?"

"Because due to my own foolishness, my own stubbornness, I almost lost you. I almost lost the best thing that has ever happened to me." He ran his hand through his hair in a gesture of distress and shook his head. "I will not let that happen again. I have not been a good mate to you, and I feel deep shame for that. You may not want to be here, but having you under my roof allows me a second chance to prove my worth to you as a mate and I will do whatever it takes to accomplish that. If I must follow you around, if I must beg you for another chance, I will. I will do either of those things—both. What I will not do, Margo, is make the same foolish mistake again. You are mine."

We stared at each other in silence. I was utterly speechless, still trying to digest what I'd just heard and reconcile it with the broody, sullen, stubborn as hell, evasive Ovide I knew. When I dropped my gaze and turned away from him, he turned also and continued into the kitchen.

I sat in stunned silence. *Beg?* Had he really used the word *beg? He* would beg *me?*

I felt a tickle on my cheek and reached up to swipe at whatever bug was crawling on me. But it wasn't a bug. Something wet had somehow splashed on my face. Tears. They were tears. I was crying.

Oh, fuck me, I never cried.

I commanded myself to nip that shit in the bud right away. *Woman up, Margo, and quit acting like a blubbering idiot.* But, instead, the tears continued to flow until I was wracked with sobs and full on bawling like a baby.

Chapter Twenty

OVIDE

I hadn't been able to rest since I found Margo in the woods. Even having Margo in my house, under my protection, didn't calm my dragon. It didn't calm me. I needed physical contact—to hold her, to feel her in my arms and not let go—for the next month or two, at least. But Margo was like a caged tiger. She was ready to lash out at anyone that got too near, especially me. It was best to give her time to cool down.

I had been the stupidest dragon that ever existed to spurn the incredible gift fate had bestowed upon me. Perhaps I felt, as the saying went, it was too good to be true.

The scent of Margo's tears hit me and I rushed back into the living room. "Are you okay? Did something happen?"

She waved me off. "I-I'm not fucking crying."

"I didn't say you were."

"Good, 'cause I'm not." She sniffled and twisted the top half of her body around to face the couch, but her leg was still stretched out. She was going to hurt it if she wasn't more careful.

"Come here." I bent down and slid my arms under her. Easily lifting her to my chest, I made sure that her leg was stable, even as her arms pushed against me.

"Put me down!" She tried half-heartedly to wriggle away from me. "I said put me down, you big dumb oaf!"

I held her tighter, my face cracking into a grin. "I will not! You are going to hurt yourself."

When I sat down with her in my lap, she behaved as though I'd dropped her into a pot of boiling water. She jerked her hips up and away from me, but I just put an arm over her to hold her still.

"Ovide! Let me go!"

"Not until you tell me what is wrong. Why are you 'not-crying'?"

She struggled stubbornly, but I could tell she was quickly depleting herself of energy. She didn't stop, though, until sweat beaded her upper lip and forehead. "Why won't you let me go?"

"Because you are going to hurt yourself. Because you cannot twist around like that. Because you cannot fight like this. Because..." I wanted to say it, to tell her that there was nothing in this world or any other that I cared more about that her, but the words that I wanted to say, the ones that were on the tip of my heart, I held back. She was not ready to hear them yet. "You are going to make your leg worse."

She finally stopped fighting, sighed and relaxed slightly against my chest. "Fine. I won't twist around. Just put me back on the couch."

I wasn't sure I was able to. Now that I had her in my arms, my dragon would not allow me to let her go. This close I could feel her heartbeat next to mine, reassuring me that she was okay. "No. Not yet."

She was frustrated, but did not resume her struggle. She even leaned her head against my shoulder. Her breathing was shallow and she used my t-shirt to wipe her face.

"I'm drugged up, or I could totally have gotten away from you."

"Doubtful. Even with two good legs."

Her human growl sent a surge of desire through my body and there was nothing I could've done to stop or to hide my erection that sprang up right under her ass. She felt it immediately and her cheeks burned bright red. Her mouth fell open and then her tongue swept out over her top lip, which hardened my cock to an even greater degree.

The desire coursing through me was demanding I take down her shorts and sink into her. I could not, no matter how much I wanted to.

It wasn't right until we sorted things out. Instead, I got up and eased her back down on the couch.

There was no way to move away without the crotch of my tented jeans being in her face, so I just plopped her down as fast as possible and stepped away to stand behind her, out of her view. "No twisting around. You will hurt yourself."

I blew out a rough breath. My dragon demanded his mate and I was hanging onto resistance by a thread. Fortunately, my brain, which still held a small semblance of sensibility, reminded me it was not the right move. Not yet.

"Are you hungry or do you want to try for that nap again?"

A few seconds passed before she answered and when she did, her voice was low and breathy. "I could eat."

I considered it a good sign that she had an appetite and quickly made roast beef sandwiches. I carried them into the living room and pulled a chair over to the couch. I took my own sandwich before handing over the plate.

I ate mine in three bites, nothing but a snack for a dragon, but Margo merely stared at hers. "You do not like roast beef sandwiches? Make a list and I will shop for you—anything you wish."

She sighed. "No, it's not that. It's...I need to go to the bathroom."

I nodded and stood. "I will carry you."

"No way. Just give me a hand up and I can do the rest."

"I will carry you."

"Back off, buster."

I removed the plate with her sandwich and sat it on the chair, fighting a grin. I doubted that there was anything in life that my fierce mate couldn't fight about. "It is the only way you are getting to the bathroom."

"I'll use the damned crutches. Don't be an ass." She tried to swing her feet off the couch and I could see the pain in her face.

I stood and easily scooped her into my arms. I took a few punches to the shoulder before growling at her to stop. "I am following the surgeon's orders. I will be carrying you back and forth for the next month. You might as well get used to it."

"Not a chance in hell! I will belly crawl out of here before I let you carry me back and forth to the bathroom for a month. Not going to happen you growly beast." She gasped when I put her down gently in front of the toilet. Her hands clenched my shoulders, fingers digging in, her face contorted in pain. "Wait. Oh, shit. Wait! Don't move, please!"

"I am not going anywhere." As soon as her breathing normalized, I ran my hands down her back and hooked her shorts and panties swiftly sliding them down to her knees, then picked her up and sat her gently on the toilet, propping her leg on a footstool.

Margo just sat there, stammering. Her face was beet red and I could practically feel her blood boiling. She was going to lay into me, but I was ready for it. "Go away! You're not going to listen to me pee too, you perv! Give a girl some privacy."

I laughed and shrugged. "Okay. I will not listen to you pee." There was no way I wouldn't hear it. Dragon senses were far keener than human. But I supposed hearing and listening were two different things. "I will step out, but do not think about getting up without me or you will get no privacy next time."

She let out a little frustrated scream and threw a roll of toilet paper at my head. "Out!"

Just outside the bathroom door, I ducked the flying toilet paper roll and tried, but failed, to keep the grin off my face. Things were definitely not going to be easy with Margo, that was certain. She never cut me any slack. And that was one of the things I loved the most about her.

And, love her I did. I loved Margo every bit as much as I cherished the memory of loving Kyrian all those years ago, because that's what Kyrian was—a memory. I realized it now. Margo was my mate. For whatever reason, fate had given me two great loves, one in the past, and one flesh and blood in the present with a promise of the future.

Armand was right. I was no longer the same dragon I was all those years ago when Kyrian and I had been young and in love. I was different. I had changed, and it was not dishonoring Kyrian's memory to continue to grow, to continue to live my life, or to be happy and in love again.

There had to be a reason fate gave me a second chance at happiness. I did not know the reason or if I deserved it, but I intended to accept it.

Chapter Twenty-One

MARGO

The big sourpuss was getting to me.

There was no way in hell I was staying with Ovide for a fucking month, though. No way in hell that I was going to have him carry me to the bathroom and pull my pants down for me like I was a toddler learning to make tinkles. Still sitting on the toilet, too embarrassed to have him come back in to help me, I decided that we were going to have it out and settle this once and for all. After I wiped and flushed, of course.

When I was ready, I crossed my arms and settled my face into my best angry glare.

Ovide stepped back inside the bathroom and a corner of his mouth lifted. "Done?"

I shook my head. "This isn't working. Call Remy and Lenni. I don't care if I cramp their newlywed style. I can't stay here."

He just leaned against the doorframe and shrugged. "You can stay here."

"No! I cannot! We had this conversation. You already have a mate, remember? Now you want to humiliate me by pulling down my pants and helping me to the bathroom."

"How is that humiliating?

"It just is. It's mortifying. No, thank you." I jabbed my finger at him, getting amped up.

He was silent for several seconds before speaking quietly. "I have no wish to humiliate you. Despite what happened, we *are* mates. It is my job to take care of you."

"Oh, wow! Now I'm your job—a chore. Wonderful. You sure know how to make a girl feel good. That's really fucking romantic!

He stood up straighter. "Is that what you want? I should be romantic? Would that make you feel better about remaining here?"

"Fuck, no. I don't know why I said that." I looked down at my bare thighs, just then realizing they were still bare and groaned then palmed my face. "This is what I'm talking about. We're arguing while I'm on the toilet. Just *no!*"

Ovide slowly made his way over to me and wrapped his arm around my waist. He lifted me with one hand, pulled my bottoms up with the other, and then scooped me up, cradling me. "Now, we can argue with you on the couch."

I shook my head. "I can't do it."

"Okay, the bed then."

I smacked him. "Don't be a smartass. You don't get it. You got to keep your pride through all of this. I didn't. I pretty much got dumped —rejected."

He put me down on the couch and sat back in the chair next to me. "I did not keep my pride through any of this."

"Bullshit. How did you *not* keep your pride?" I crossed my arms over my chest and stared at him defiantly.

"I have been a complete fool. Worse than a fool and I am filled with shame."

"You are?" I softened a little.

"I am. A dragon's biggest duty in his life—his greatest honor—is keeping his mate safe and happy. Protecting her, caring for her, honoring her. I cannot even begin to explain the layers of how I messed that up."

I relaxed my defensive posture slightly. "You did mess that up."

The set of his jaw was grim. "I thought I was letting my mate down —and I was. I was just too foolish to realize that it was *you* I was letting down, Margo, not Kyrian. Kyrian no longer needs me. This isn't supposed to happen. Fate doesn't give dragons two mates. I thought it was a mistake."

My heart ached, but I listened to every word like it would be the last. "And now? Do you still think we're a mistake?"

"I thought I was the only one who was feeling hurt and confused. I did not try hard enough to consider your feelings and you almost died because of that."

"Is that why you want me now? You feel guilty that I almost died?"

He leaned forward in his seat and shook his head. "No. I mean, yes. I do feel guilty. That's not why I'm asking you to stay here."

"Asking is not what you're doing, but okay."

"Kyrian's face started fading from my head the moment I saw you. I can barely remember it now. My dragon... He's obsessed with you. He's moved on. I can't deny what fate has put in front of me. I don't understand it. You're so different from her. You get under my skin, frustrate me, anger me."

"Extreme romance happening here, huh?"

"That. You're so ready to fight. You want to fight me constantly. I think you'd rather stab me in the eye than talk to me most of the time. I've never felt anything like it. I don't get you at all, but I can't get you out of my head." He rubbed his hands over his face. "When Kyrian died... I thought my world was over. I don't know how I lived through it day after day, month after month, year after year. I planted an entire forest in her memory as I waited to die. It never happened, though.

"When I found you in the forest and I thought you were dying, I felt intense regret. I think I stayed alive to find you. I don't understand this all. Maybe you and I are supposed to argue with one another for the rest of our lives or something. I don't know. I just know that I would not have survived burying you."

I pressed my back into the couch hard, searching for some kind of stability. "I don't know how to believe you. You wanted nothing to do with me."

"I was wrong."

Those three simple words made more sense than anything else he'd ever said. I latched onto them. "You were wrong. And now..."

"Now, I am right again." He gave me a lopsided grin. "You know about mates. Even though we do not fit the rules, I think everything else is the same."

"I don't know about any of this. I kind of lost my sanity over it. I tried to find you in the middle of the night, all to demand that you either accept me as your mate or kill me. Do you understand that? I wanted to die."

"I would rather kill myself a million times over. If you give me another chance, I will never allow you to feel that way again. I promise."

"It scares me. *You* scare me." I looked away.

He took my hand. "I don't have all the answers, but I will not be running from fate again."

I hated the excitement that was budding in my chest. Hope. That was what I was feeling. Could it actually work? I looked down at the cast on my leg. Time was all I had until I got that fucker off.

I looked up at Ovide, who met my gaze and leaned back in the chair as he waited for me to respond.

"Fine."

"Fine, what?"

I crossed my arms again and scowled at him, needing to distance myself from all the emotional stuff. "Fine, maybe we can give it a shot —the getting to know each other part. I don't have anything better to do for the next month, anyway."

Chapter Twenty-Two

MARGO

"You're cheating! You can't just keep all of the cards like that! That is not how you play the game!" I threw my cards down and groaned. "You're doing that on purpose, aren't you? Because you know it drives me crazy."

Ovide gave me a dark grin and gathered the cards to shuffle again. "I do not know what you're talking about."

I narrowed my eyes at him and grabbed the pillow next to me to hit him with. He caught it and tossed it back at me. "You never play fair. It makes me crazy. *You* make me crazy."

"There is a lot of talk about you being crazy. I suppose, as your mate, I must agree with you. It is only right." He met my eyes with a challenge in his. They sparkled with mischief.

My body reacted instantly. That wasn't new. It'd been a week since I'd arrived at Ovide's, a week since we decided to get to know each other better. It'd been a constant barrage of feelings. Ovide came out of his cranky, doom-and-gloom shell and the man I met was unlike any other. The sly smiles and playfulness hit me in all the right places, while also making me want to strangle him. He didn't back down from my anger or bossiness. He challenged me back and I couldn't remember any other man ever doing it the way he did.

"Play another?"

I looked him over and sighed. "Fine. If you cheat again, I'm going to flip this table, though."

"As though you could." He reached over and squeezed my bicep. "I'm not sure that these noodles are not just for looks."

I flexed my muscle and scowled. "You want to see me flip the table?"

"Yes, I do." He picked the cards up and sat back with his arms crossed over his chest. His easy challenge was infuriating and he knew it. "Go ahead."

I held his gaze, meeting his challenge with one of my own. Reaching down, I grabbed the table and was about to flip the hell out of that mother fucker when voices floated in through the front screen door.

Ovide planted his hand in the middle of the table and leaned over it, his face dangerously close to mine. "Saved by the annoying bunch."

I wanted to grab the sides of his face and kiss him—but I didn't. We hadn't touched more than necessary in the week that had passed, despite how badly my desire for him grew. Somehow, we'd gone into a stalemate—neither of us pushing too far. It had become a challenge of who would crack first. I didn't know for sure if he was playing the same game, but I was determined to see him lose control first.

"Try to contain your disappointment at having to share me." I smirked and leaned back on the couch.

He reached out and stroked a finger down my cheek. "I do not share."

Once again, I was left breathless as Lenni and Nance burst in. They visited every day, bringing gifts each time. It was too much, but they insisted.

"Good news!" Lenni rushed into the living room and gave Ovide a look before taking his chair and sitting across from me. "You get to get out of the house next week. You have a check-up with the orthopedic surgeon. I pretended to be you and scheduled it for you."

I shrugged. "I'm not sure a doctor's appointment is good news."

"I think I know what will pep you right up." Nance wagged her eyebrows. "A little wham-bam from dragon-man."

I heard Ovide chuckle from the kitchen and glared at Nance. "Shut up."

Lenni rolled her eyes. "Are you two still not boinking? That's insane. What are you waiting for?"

I was going to kill both of them. "What day is the doctor's appointment?"

"Seriously, it's not like your leg should keep you from having sex. We looked up some positions for couples when one has a broken leg. There are some really fun ones."

Something crashed in the kitchen and Nance reached over to silently high-five Lenni. "Just go for it. After what you said about how good it was the first time, I'm shocked you can keep your hands off of him."

I wasn't just going to kill them. No, no, I was going to torture them slowly and then kill them. They were going to regret butting their noses into my business.

"We brought your bath stuff. The doctor told you...er...me...that you could take a bath finally. No more sponging yourself clean. Just keep your leg out of the water. It shouldn't be hard with Ovide to help." Lenni dropped a bag at my feet. She grinned wickedly and I wondered where my sweet, innocent friend had gone. "I also packed your favorite lingerie. You know, the black lace pieces?"

"It's time for you two to go now." I shook my head at them and pointed at the door. "Both of you. Out!"

"We get it. It's time to spend some real *quality* time with your mate, huh?"

I mouthed a threat to them and growled in frustration when they just laughed and waved goodbye. I heard them whispering to Ovide in the kitchen. There was no telling what they were saying to him. If I'd been able to get up and move, I would've unleashed some sophisticated martial arts moves on all three.

Ovide came back into the room a few minutes later, holding a packet of papers in his hand. "They gave me a list of different positions to use for sexual intercourse when one partner has a broken leg, complete with written instructions as well as sketches on the mechanics of each position."

I squeezed my eyes shut and nodded. "Yeah."

"It is a very comprehensive list." When my eyes flew open and went to his, I found him grinning.

He was toying with me and, as infuriating as it was, it turned me on. "Really nice."

"Wow. This one... *Whew.*" He dropped into his chair across from me and used the papers to fan himself dramatically, still grinning at me. "Creative. Some of these..." He furrowed his brows and turned the stack of papers sideways studying it. "Hmm. I don't believe this female's leg is really broken."

I sat up and tried to snatch the papers away from him. The idea of him looking at another woman fueled the green-eyed monster in me. I didn't like it. "I've already started a list of people I'm going to murder when I get my leg back. You want your name at the top?"

"With those noodle arms?"

I glared at him.

He stood up and smiled down at me, the picture of ease. I could see the lust in his eyes, though. He was close to losing control. Just a little push...

"I think I'm ready for my bath. Did you hear? The doctor cleared me for it. I'll need help, though."

He nodded. "You will need help."

I nodded with an exaggerated sigh. "It's too bad Lenni and Nance already left."

"Are you sure we shouldn't play a couple more games first?"

I shrugged. "It's up to you."

A beat passed before he shoved the table out of the way and lifted me into his arms. He didn't mention the way my breath hitched when he touched me. I didn't mention his massive erection resting just under my ass.

More than the tension, there was something that had bloomed between us. Something that until now had stayed just under the surface but had been present since our first night together.

I knew him better now. I liked his quick wit and intensity. I liked the way he teased me, but watched me to make sure it wasn't too much. In the span of a week, he'd accomplished making me feel that with him, I had a home.

It was terrifying for me, but I knew when I looked into his eyes that he was just as scared, and I was ready for us to take this thing all the way.

Chapter Twenty-Three
OVIDE

As the tub filled, I dragged my shirt over my head and tossed it aside. The game of keep-away was over. I did not want to tease my little mate anymore. I wanted to devour her. I'd kept my hands to myself for the entire week, but the smell of her arousal had been filling my head nonstop.

She raised her arms and sank her teeth into her lower lip. Her eyes were burning pools of emeralds as she raked them over my chest. I caught the hem of her shirt and let my fingertips drag up her sides and down her arms as I pulled it off. Her bare breasts heaved up and down with rough breaths.

I drank her in and growled. *Perfect.* I unbuttoned my pants. Her throat worked and she let out what sounded like a little purr.

That one sound brought me to my knees in front of her. I leaned forward and pressed my lips to the top of her bare thigh. Gripping the waistband of her shorts, I pulled them down and carefully moved them over her cast. Her panties next, she was bare in front of me, her shoulders back and that chin raised. Instead of defiance, I saw hunger in her.

Her fingers grasped the zipper of my pants and worked it down.

Then, slowly, she pushed my pants down. She let out another one of those sounds when my dick sprang free.

I kicked off my pants but didn't give her a chance to explore my body. Not yet. Picking her up, I stepped into the tub and sank into the water carefully resting her body against mine, leaving her leg propped on the edge of the tub on a folded towel. The cleft of her ass cradled my cock, her soft skin slick against my chest. The steamy water sloshed around us and I wrapped my arms around her waist, content to hold her for the moment.

She leaned her head back against my shoulder and turned to look up at me, waiting.

I took the soap from the edge of the tub and lathered it in my hands. Starting at her shoulders, I massaged her tight muscles while washing her. Down her arms, over her stomach, I lathered and stroked her everywhere except where she wanted me to.

When I couldn't keep my hands away, I cupped her breasts and took my time soaping her nipples and stroking her slippery skin. I worked my hands down her stomach and cupped her sex which elicited a soft moan. Her hips rocked against me, but I just held her. Her grunt of frustration made me chuckle. Her small hand moved over mine and pressed down on my fingers. Slipping through her wet folds, I let her use my hand to pleasure herself. She moved my fingertip over her clit in tight circles, and I listened closely to her breathing until I heard it coming in little gasps. She was already close.

Not yet, though. I pulled my hand away and slid her forward enough to lay her head back so that her hair fell into the water. She grunted in frustration, but I quieted her displeasure by working shampoo into her hair and massaging her scalp. Her hair stroked over my cock and I fought for my control while I continued to wash her.

It was a game of torture for both of us. When I had her back against my chest, clean and wet all over, we were both breathing heavily and wiggling against each other.

"Ovide..." Her voice was breathless and her hand snaked behind my neck and held me. "Stop fucking torturing me."

I buried my face in the crook of her neck and forced the words out. "My mate. *Mine*."

She heard the slight questioning tone in that statement and her hand tightened on the back of my neck. "You sure about that?"

I lifted her hips and she angled them until the head of my cock brushed her opening. I pulled her down slowly, impaling her with my shaft inch by inch. She locked her other hand behind my neck, too, and forced her body the rest of the way down. Her back was arched, her breasts thrust forward.

Even with her leg sticking out of the water, Margo's physical strength was impressive. She lifted her hips and slid back down, fucking herself on me. I cupped her breasts and growled into the shell of her ear as her body worked me over. Up and down, her core milked me. When she slowed down, I dropped one hand to her hips and did the work for her.

She was close. I could feel her orgasm tightening her body. Dropping my hand to her small nub, I rubbed it the way she liked and thrust into her. The angle changed slightly, hitting just the right way. Her nails scored my neck as her tight core pulsed around me. Just as her orgasm started, I scraped my teeth down her throat and then sank them into her neck as I had that first night.

Completely connected, I felt the first wave of my orgasm hit. Stronger than anything I'd ever felt, I sank my teeth in farther, desperate to mark her through and through. I needed her to know that, while the first time might not have been completely intentional, this one was. Her blood exploded in my mouth as we reached our climaxes together. Drunk on her, I tossed my head back and let out a wild roar.

Margo, my wild little mate, tipped her head back and let out her own little human roar. Her body still pulsed around mine, her nails still imbedded in my neck, she let her head roll to the side. "Okay, yours."

I growled and ran my tongue over her mark. "Mine. Forever."

I was still needy for her, and still hard. I was mindful of her leg, though. Our skin was pruning from the cooling water and I was sure that if I did not tend to her, her leg would begin hurting soon. I didn't want to move, but her needs came first.

I eased us out of the tub and placed her on the counter while I dried her flushed body off. She watched as I dried off and then wrapped herself around me as I carried her to my bed.

"Do not tell Lenni and Nance that they goaded us into that. I'll never hear the end of it"

I settled on my side, staring down at her. Stroking her stomach, my mind filled with visions of it filled with young. I smiled. "I would not dream of it."

She reached up and stroked her finger over my cheek. "I heard that."

I nodded. "I said it aloud."

She shook her head. "No. I heard your thoughts—about babies."

Blinking, I was stunned. I was afraid that it would scare her away. The past week had taken me over the hurdle of living in the past. I knew what I wanted. Kyrian would always have a place in my heart, but fate had brought me Margo and she was my future. I wanted a future with her—one that included younglings with her fierce, fiery attitude. I worried that she hadn't gotten there, though.

"If I didn't think it would swell your head up to the size of a small state, I would tell you that I love you." She said it casually and looked up at the ceiling.

A smile broke out on my face. "If I didn't think you'd threaten to kill me over it, I would tell you that I love you, too."

"So, are we a thing now?" She gestured between us. "We're doing this? This mate thing?"

I laughed, suddenly feeling a hundred years younger. "Oh, yes. This is happening."

Chapter Twenty-Four

OVIDE

The first rays of morning light were just beginning to stream into the bedroom. My beautiful mate slept beside me, her head on the pillow, her flaming red hair fanned out over the pillowcase. My soul soared at the thought that I would do this every morning—awaken to the sight of Margo beside me.

I had, however, learned not to take such things for granted. I would cherish her for the rest of my days. But, one never knew how many days one had, so it was best to live each one extracting every ounce of happiness possible.

I had no desire to leave the bed or my mate's side, but I had unfinished business. There was one thing I had yet to do. I had promised Margo I would honor her and try my hardest to be a mate worthy of her and I intended to keep that promise.

Quietly, I rose and dressed. As I stepped out onto the back porch, the grass was damp with dew that glistened in the rising sun's light. I took a breath of fresh morning air. It promised to be a hot, muggy day, as was usual for the time of year, but the morning was pleasant. I took a moment to remain on the porch and gaze out one last time at the tree line, just as I had year after year, decade after decade. It looked different today. Or, maybe it was me that was different.

The smaller saplings were in front, but behind them, the trees grew increasingly larger. They had been such a part of my life for so long. Each and every tree, a token. Some having stood for almost a hundred years—month after month, year after year as a memorial, a testament to my mourning, my sorrow, and my loneliness.

I no longer felt loneliness or sorrow. I was in mourning no longer.

I stepped off the porch and strode quickly to the small lean-to which held my maintenance equipment. It was the chainsaw I was after.

As I fueled it up, I tried to estimate how long it would take to level the entire forest. It could take a few days and then there was the matter of removing the felled trees.

"Just what the hell are you doing?"

I swung around at the question to find Margo standing in the damp grass, sleepy-eyed and barefoot, with a sheet wrapped around her. I had been so engrossed in my thoughts I hadn't heard her approach. The question was not surprising. What was surprising was that the tone of her voice was not inquisitive. She sounded horrified.

"I am honoring you, my mate, as I promised."

"With a fucking chainsaw? You're planning to cut those trees down, aren't you?"

I frowned. Why did she sound upset? "I am."

Her eyes narrowed. "Why?"

"Because they were planted in memory of another female and you should not have to live in another's shadow."

Her forehead wrinkled. "Another's shadow? Is that what I'm doing? Am I overshadowed by Kyrian in your mind?"

"No! You are my world, Margo. Kyrian is my past. My memories."

She threw her hands up forgetting she had been holding the sheet around her and had to grab it quickly before it fell to the ground. "Exactly! And I don't expect you to give up your past! Or saw it down. Your past is what made you who you are."

I was confused. I thought she would be glad to see me remove the trees, my monument to Kyrian. Why wouldn't she? As I stood confused and unsure of what to say next, she blew out a slow breath. "I know you loved Kyrian."

"Yes. The boy I was loved her very deeply."

She nodded. "And the man?"

"The man I am loves *you*. Very deeply."

"See? I know that." Margo stepped forward and slid the chainsaw out of my hand. She turned and placed it back into the lean-to. "You know what I see when I look at those trees?"

I shrugged, completely baffled.

"I see a man who loves so fiercely, so devotedly, that his heartache built an entire forest. And I know that man loves me with that same fierce devotion. When I look at those trees, they remind me of how lucky I am to have scored that guy. I don't need you to erase your past —I don't want you to. That would mean erasing a part of you and I want to keep you the way you are—all of you."

I wrapped her in my arms and held her close, breathing in her morning scent of pineapple and coconut. "As long as you know there is nothing for you to feel threatened about. You are my everything."

She smiled her glowing smile. "I know that." Then, she shuddered. "I wouldn't mind if you ridded the place of wolves, though."

I already had. It had been just the one lone wolf and I hadn't enjoyed killing the animal, but my dragon would settle for nothing less after it had injured our mate. Besides, I couldn't risk it ever going after her or anyone else again.

"You want to honor me? Take me back to bed. Your mate needs a big, hot dragon-man and a little morning sex."

She needn't say another word. I scooped her up and headed back into the house marveling at the petite firecracker in my arms. My mate was truly the strongest, fiercest, bravest warrior I had ever known.

Chapter Twenty-Five

MARGO

Another day, another dragon gang party. They loved any chance to get together and celebrate. This time it was a graduation party for Sky's nephew, Nick. The whole gang was in the party room of The Gator Pit. Even some of Nick's friends were there.

Thankfully, I was finally out of my cast. My leg had a faint scar as a reminder, but that was it. In a cute sundress and my heavy boots, I was unashamedly sitting in Ovide's lap.

Chyna and Cherry and Angel, their mates beside them, were giggling and swapping baby stories. Sky and Beast had just announced that they were pregnant to all of us and everyone was excited. Nick would be going off to college in the fall, a whole year early, but he'd already committed to somewhere close, not wanting to be too far away from the new baby when it came.

I looked across the room and met Lenni's eyes. She was glowing, happier than I'd ever seen her. She'd progressed so far from the woman who almost married an asshole to please her family.

From what I understood, just a year and a half prior, all the dragon guys had been single and living their lives under the threat of some eclipse coming and wiping them out. How things had changed.

Sky stood. "I won't make a big deal out of this, but I just wanted to say that I'm so proud of you, Nick. Graduating early is huge and you made it look easy. Beast and I couldn't have asked for better boys to raise than you and Casey." Sky's face was split into a huge grin, her pride obvious. "But you're still not getting a car."

Nick groaned. "Great. I'll drive your pride to college."

Everyone laughed.

Suddenly, Ovide's thoughts entered my head. *Want to sneak into your office for a couple orgasms?* His hand snaked higher on my thigh, his fingertips slipping under my dress.

I grinned. *You givin' or gettin'?*

Both.

Sounds good, I waggled my brows, *as long as you bring a slice of that cake with you.* He stood up and put me on my feet. "I would never argue with my woman."

I laughed, rolling my eyes. "You're full of shit. You argue with me all the time."

I was reaching for his hand to drag him away when someone shouted from the main area that there was a fight. Some things never changed.

"Margo..."

I was already on my way to break it up. I didn't need Ovide to step in for me. I was a grown ass woman who'd been handling my own shit for long enough to know that I didn't need his help. But I let him help anyway since I had learned that he could be an excellent bouncer.

I found a couple of college aged guys fighting and made quick work of breaking it up. When they tried to go back at each other, I stepped in between them and growled. I'd learned some tips from Ovide on how to perfect my 'human growl', as he called it.

"The next one of you who touches the other one will lose a body part. My choice. You think I'm kidding? Try me." I gave them my meanest stink-eyed glare. "Hold your liquor better or don't fucking come back. I've got better things to do than come out here and deal with a couple of jack-offs."

They didn't look scared enough, so I glanced over my shoulder. I knew Ovide was right behind me. On cue, he let out a ferocious growl.

I jerked my thumb back at Ovide. "If I'm not scary enough for you, my guy will eat you in one bite. Literally."

That worked like a charm and both the guys looked down at the floor in submission.

I nodded at Devon, my new bartender, and Ovide frowned.

"Who is that male? I have not seen him here before."

"That's my new bartender. I've been slowly hiring more help so I'll have enough staff to take over for me when I'm on maternity leave."

Ovide nodded, the gist of my words not yet sinking in.

Suddenly, his eyes widened. "Maternity..."

I nodded. "Yep. Turns out unprotected sex leads to little dragon babies pretty quickly. You'd think we would've learned from all the rest of the knocked-up dragon gang."

He lifted me and grabbed my ass so I'd wrap my legs around his waist. "My mate is with young?"

I nodded as he carried me through the crowd ignoring everyone else in the room. He didn't stop until we were in my office.

"You better lock the door, Ovide."

He kicked the door closed and locked it. I laughed as he lowered me onto my desk and slowly slid my skirt up. "Damn. I forgot to grab cake."

The End.

P.O.L.A.R.

(**P**rivate **O**ps: **L**eague **A**rctic **R**escue) is a specialized, private operations task force—a maritime unit of polar bear shifters. Part of a world-wide, clandestine army comprised of the best of the best shifters, P.O.L.A.R.'s home base is Siberia...until the team pisses somebody off and gets re-assigned to Sunkissed Key, Florida and these arctic shifters suddenly find themselves surrounded by sun, sand, flip-flops and palm trees.

1. Rescue Bear
2. Hero Bear
3. Covert Bear
4. Tactical Bear
5. Royal Bear

———

BEARS OF BURDEN

In the southwestern town of Burden, Texas, good ol' bears Hawthorne, Wyatt, Hutch, Sterling, and Sam, and Matt are livin' easy. Beer flows freely, and pretty women are abundant. The last thing the shifters of Burden are thinking about is finding a mate or settling down. But, fate has its own plan...

1. Thorn
2. Wyatt
3. Hutch
4. Sterling
5. Sam
6. Matt

———

SHIFTERS OF HELL'S CORNER

In the late 1800's, on a homestead in New Mexico, a female shifter named Helen Cartwright, widowed under mysterious circumstances, knew there was power in the feminine bonds of sisterhood. She provided an oasis for those like herself, women who had been dealt the short end of the stick. Like magic, women have flocked to the tiny town of Helen's Corner ever since. Although, nowadays, some call the town by another name, **Hell's Crazy Corner.**

1. Wolf Boss
2. Wolf Detective
3. Wolf Soldier
4. Bear Outlaw
5. Wolf Purebred

––––––

DRAGONS OF THE BAYOU

Something's lurking in the swamplands of the Deep South. Massive creatures exiled from their home. For each, his only salvation is to find his one true mate.

1. Fire Breathing Beast
2. Fire Breathing Cezar
3. Fire Breathing Blaise
4. Fire Breathing Remy
5. Fire Breathing Armand
6. Fire Breathing Ovide

––––––

RANCHER BEARS

When the patriarch of the Long family dies, he leaves a will that has each of his five son's scrambling to find a mate. Underneath it all, they find that family is what matters most.

1. Rancher Bear's Baby
2. Rancher Bear's Mail Order Mate
3. Rancher Bear's Surprise Package
4. Rancher Bear's Secret
5. Rancher Bear's Desire
6. Rancher Bears' Merry Christmas

Rancher Bears Complete Box Set

———

KODIAK ISLAND SHIFTERS

On Port Ursa in Kodiak Island Alaska, the Sterling brothers are kind of a big deal.
They own a nationwide chain of outfitter retail stores that they grew from their father's little backwoods camping supply shop.
The only thing missing from the hot bear shifters' lives are mates! But, not for long...

1. Billionaire Bear's Bride (COLTON)
2. The Bear's Flamingo Bride (WYATT)
3. Military Bear's Mate (TUCKER)

———

SHIFTERS OF DENVER

Nathan: Billionaire Bear‑ A matchmaker meets her match.
Byron: Heartbreaker Bear‑ A sexy heartbreaker with eyes for just one woman.
Xavier: Bad Bear ‑ She's a good girl. He's a bad bear.

1. Nathan: Billionaire Bear
2. Byron: Heartbreaker Bear
3. Xavier: Bad Bear

Shifters of Denver Complete Box Set

Printed in Great Britain
by Amazon

38955220R00073